I0557128

Benito

S.W. Campbell

Published by Shawn Campbell

This is a work of fiction. Unless otherwise indicated, all the names, characters, businesses, places, events and incidents in this book are either the product of the author's imagination or used in a fictitious manner. Any resemblance to actual persons, living or dead, or actual events is purely coincidental.

Benito

ISBN: 979-8-9870287-9-7

To Bill, my grandfather, for going overseas to serve his country and fight the Nazis.

Benito

Part 1 - Il Bivio

I could tell that the Lyft driver was getting nervous because he kept bringing up the fact that he kept a .45 under his seat.

"Not loaded," he said with what I took to be false bravado. "I'm scared to death I'll hit a bad bump and shoot a toe off or something, but the magazine is in the glove box and I can get it ready to go faster than you can say my slap happy pappy has a crap happy grandpappy."

"That seems like quite the mouthful," I answered, a bit incredulously.

I expected him to say something like that's what your momma says, because he seemed like the type, but evidently he wasn't all that clever.

"I'm a Second Amendment man," he declared.

"I'm more of a Third Amendment man myself," I answered.

"Pardon?"

From the look he gave me in the rearview mirror he was obviously confused.

"It wouldn't work out," I answered, "my apartment just isn't that big."

I won't bore you with all of the lengthy conversation I had with this particular Lyft driver. Everything from why the cars no longer have to have the pink moustache on them, to his favorite kinds of salted cured meats, capocollo being an especial favorite, to his evidently very strong opinions regarding newscasters with a prominent vocal fry. To be fair, as I said before, he was obviously nervous, and lots of people are talkers when they're nervous. After all, we were going to a crossroads far out in the middle of nowhere in the very early morning, though I guess it wasn't nowhere for the people in the area, I'm guessing pretty few judging by the lack of other vehicles or house lights. Either way, it was kind of funny. Given I'm such a slight person it was hard to imagine anybody finding me all that intimidating.

The distant sky was just beginning to have a purplish Midwestern haze when the driver's phone announced we were mere minutes from our destination. I had a twinge of conscience.

"Look," I said to the eyes watching me in the rearview mirror, "I need to level with you. I'm out here to meet old Jumpin' Jack Flash to make a deal."

The eyes narrowed.

"This better not be a drug deal. It's against the terms and conditions of my contract with Lyft to be involved in that kind of shit."

"No narcotics," I promised, "I'm out here meeting Old Scratch if you catch my drift."

The driver grunted in response.

"If it was me, I'd look into getting friends with normal names who don't ask to meet in out of the way places so early in the butt fucking morning."

We stopped about fifty yards from the crossroads. There was nothing but long rows of immature corn around us, black in the twilight, latched to the horizon by distant lines of shadowed trees.

"Stay here and wait for me," I told the driver.

"I can't be involved in illegal activity of any kind. My contract..."

"I'm not buying or selling narcotics," I promised.

"Whatever," he answered.

A tall wooden signpost stood at the corner, none of the lettering directing me back to Chicago, though if I turned around I would have undoubtedly seen its light on the horizon. I got out of the car and started making my way down the gravel road toward the meeting spot. The Devil hadn't yet arrived.

That's right, I actually was out there to meet the Devil, hard as it might be to believe. My buddy Teddy hooked me up. Teddy knows all sorts of people.

"Of course I know him," Teddy had said with a braggadocious tone of voice. "I just sold an old dirt bike to him last month."

Teddy had given me directions on how to get things set up. He didn't even ask me why I wanted to meet with the Devil in the first place. Teddy was good like that.

I got up to the crossroads and was just standing there, waiting, shivering a bit in the cold morning air, and eventually feeling kind of foolish, like haha, way to go Teddy, you really got me you fricking bastard, when as casual as you please out pops this guy from behind the signpost. This was pretty impressive given it was no thicker than my forearm. The signpost that is, not the guy. This was pretty impressive given working out is not exactly on the top of my to do list.

He wasn't quite as I imagined him, and I doubt I would have believed it myself if he hadn't just appeared right in front of me, seemingly out of nowhere. He was kind of a weaselly looking fella with a shaved head and one of those long chin beards like Scott Ian from Anthrax. He was wearing a black pleather vest hanging open over a white t-shirt covered in yellow stains, I want to say chicken satay maybe, ratty old dungarees, and those kind of boots that look like work boots but are actually super expensive and wouldn't last a day if you tried to do any actual work in them. He also had the start of a beer belly, like the baby bump of a woman three months pregnant, which I know because that was the point all the women I hung out with in my twenties quit hanging out with me. All except Emily, who instead of opting for a baby bump decided instead to get six to eight abortions, which don't get me wrong, I'm very pro-choice, but might be a few too many if you know what I mean.

But I digress. Regarding the Devil's appearance, luckily for me I had gone through a leather daddy phase and been to Burning Man the year it rained really hard, so I wasn't easily intimidated.

"Are you Old Scratch?"

"I prefer Harry," replied the Devil.

He had the voice of a used car salesman. Even from a distance, his breath stank of brimstone and Cool Ranch Doritos.

"I've never heard you called Harry."

"I think it's kind of a Dorset thing."

"Where the hell is Dorset?" I asked.

"Please mind your language," he replied.

We stood there, just looking at each other. The Devil chewed off one of his fingernails and spit it onto the gravel where it caught fire.

"So, you're looking to make a deal," said the Devil in a rather matter of fact way.

"That's right," I replied, trying to sound casual about it. "I want..."

He cut me off.

"I know what you want."

4

Of course he knew what I wanted, after all, he was the Devil, but I guess I should at least tell you what I wanted, because otherwise that's all you're going to be thinking about instead of listening to the rest of my damn story.

I was there to ask the Devil to give me the role of Captain Hook at the local repertory theater adaptation of Peter fricking Pan. I know, it's fricking ridiculous, but you try being nothing more than the understudy to Mindy Gabaldon for ten years running and tell me you wouldn't do the same. Fricking Mindy Gabaldon, queen of the local arts scene and seemingly blessed with the health of a damn horse. When we did South Pacific, I had to play a damn palm tree, seriously, a damn palm tree, because her fricking brother, Greg Gabaldon, our perpetual director, didn't want to risk having to swap around too many important parts in case Mindy got sick or something. Which is a bunch of bullshit of course, all of it just being politics, you know, me not being part of the good old boys' clubs that run such things.

"So do we have a deal then?" I demanded.

"Couldn't you just Tonya Harding her or something? You know..."

The Devil mimed whacking a knee with a pipe.

"I'm not a violent person," I answered.

"I see." He kicked a bit of gravel with his boot. "Well, here's the thing, you really don't have much of anything I really want."

"Excuse me?" I felt rather offended. "Is this because I'm queer?"

The Devil looked rather uncomfortable, raising his hands up in protest.

"Nobody gives a darn about that. Not me, not the people upstairs. It's just that your soul is not exactly in mint condition, and if I'm being honest, I'm probably just going to end up with it anyways."

Well, what could I say? I mean, anybody who knew me in my younger years would have to agree that it was probably a fair assertion.

"Then what the hell am I supposed to do?"

I was letting my frustration fully shine through.

"Watch your language," reminded the Devil.

We stared at each other. He just shrugged and mimed swinging a pipe again. I'm not proud, but I started to cry. That real ugly kind of cry where you try to hold it back, but it just makes it so much worse.

"This isn't fair," I blubbered.

"That's not my doing."

I just kept crying, tears and snot flowing downwards. From the look on his face, the Devil was pretty uncomfortable with such a show of emotion. He must not have had an emotionally vulnerable father figure in his upbringing.

"Look," he finally said, or something like that. I'm not a fricking recording device. "I don't want your soul, but maybe I'll throw you a bone if you buy a soul off of me?"

"Excuse me?"

I was so surprised I stopped my bawling, which if you know me, once I start I rarely stop until I'm done.

"I've got a soul I've been trying to offload for a while now. You buy it from me and I'll take care of your whole Mindy Gabadalacious or whoever as a favor."

I was instantly suspicious, you know, because it was the fricking Devil.

"How much do I have to pay?"

"However much you have on you."

The Devil smirked a bit at me expectantly, but I paid it no mind. This was a bit of a break. I rarely carried much cash on me.

"Whose soul?"

I was still very much suspicious.

"Benito Mussolini," he answered matter of factly.

"The fascist dictator?"

The Devil pointed finger guns at me and made a clicking noise out of the side of his mouth.

"Yeah, that's the one."

I was puzzled.

"You would think he would be right up your alley."

The Devil rolled his eyes.

"He's so annoying. The guy is always bouncing off the damn walls and he constantly talks about himself in this bombastic self-aggrandizing manner. I conquered Ethiopia! I conquered Albania! I have larger than average sized genitalia! I mean c'mon, he was a tiny guy with a big head who ended up naked and hanging upside down at a gas station! Big whoop!"

The Devil paused to calm himself a bit.

"Plus he's a filthy Italian," he added.

I rocked a bit back and forward on my heels.

"That sounds a bit bigoted."

"Well, I am the Devil."

"Fair," I said.

"Is it a deal?"

"Do Italians just not go to Hell then?"

I should probably mention that I have a bit of a problem with keeping my mouth shut. Emily calls me Sherlock Groans because I always ask one question too many. I don't think it's that funny, but she's also told me that her jokes are meant to entertain her, not me.

The Devil kicked a little rock over with his fancy boot, scuffing it a bit.

"We mostly stick the bad ones in purgatory for eternity," he answered. "Them and Latvians. I really dislike Latvians, but that's more of a personal thing."

"I see," I said.

"Do we have a deal or not?"

I mean, what else was I supposed to do? It wasn't like I had a lot of other options, you know, other than just walking away, but I didn't get up at the ass crack of dawn to not get what I wanted most in the world.

"Sure," I said, taking out my wallet and pulling out the fourteen bucks it contained.

"Give me that Subway card too," he demanded.

"I've got a six inch coming my way."

"You want the deal or not?" he growled.

I handed over the Subway card.

"Sweet," he said. "I'm going to get me a Seafood Sensation."

And with that, he reached behind him and pulled out an old pint bottle of Jose Cuervo from who knows where, holding it gingerly between two fingers as though even touching it disgusted him. The bottle looked vintage. The label was half rubbed off.

"What's this?"

"It's the soul."

He answered with a wink, which left me wondering whether or not it was true. I mean, the liquid in the bottle looked a bit cloudy, but otherwise no different than any other tequila I had ever seen.

"Are you sure?" I was a bit incredulous.

"What do you want, like a bejeweled crystal decanter or something?"

I took the bottle. The Devil pulled an old beat up dirt bike out from behind the signpost. His foot rammed down on the kick starter. The bike sputtered but didn't start. He tried again with the same result.

"Do you need help?" I asked.

The Devil was fiddling with the choke.

"I've got it," he answered.

Another attempt failed.

"Maybe you flooded it," I suggested, not really sure what it meant but knowing it had something to do with motorcycles.

"It's a new bike," tried to explain the Devil, "at least new to me."

He tried again. The bike roared to life with a plume of black oily smoke. He flashed me a victorious grin and then slipped the clutch. The bike jerked forward and nearly died again, but he saved it with a sudden romp on the throttle that scattered gravel behind him as he careened wildly down the road. I watched him go, cradling the bottle in my arms.

Benito

Part 2 - Il Mio Patto

Of course the Lyft driver left my ass, earning himself one star and a pretty harsh review, so I had to walk a couple miles until somebody finally picked me up, a nice old hippie lady named Jenna who had a sticker for a twenty-year old election on the bumper of her Subaru.

"Pretty early to start," she said when she saw the bottle in my hand.

I thought about telling her that I was holding the eternal soul of the founder of fascism, but instead just went with a joke instead.

"Or pretty late to stop now."

She laughed and gave Orland Square Mall where I could catch a bus back into the city. By the time I got home it was late morning, so I stuck the Benito bottle behind a bunch of others on my liquor shelf, because it didn't seem like something to just leave lying around, and went back to bed.

Well, it wasn't before too long that I was awakened by a knocking on my door, that turned out to be Agatha Christie. She wasn't the real Agatha Christie of course. She was just my elderly cleaning lady who kind of looked like

Agatha Christie, so that's how I refer to her to people who aren't her. I had forgotten it was the day she was supposed to be cleaning my apartment.

"Hello Annis," I said when I answered the door, Annis being her actual name.

"Cleaning time, ya wanker," she declared in her thick English accent.

Agatha Christie is actually English, unlike many of those fakers you meet in the repertory theater world, though it was working class English, not that fancy aristocratic English. From Devonshire, she says, though I have no idea if that's true or if it's even a real place, English geography not really being of much interest to me.

"Ya look like a well pumped cunt today," she said.

Did I mention that she's kind of an old bitch?

"Do I?"

"You have the mug of a homosexual," she added.

Also there's that. Though A) what does that even mean, and B) while it is definitely offensive she does do a great job cleaning at pretty low rates, and C) I guess it technically doesn't refer exactly to me given I'm not technically homosexual, but more like David Bowie, you know, not homosexual or heterosexual, just sexual, but still, c'mon Agatha, get your shit together.

"About me rates," she said, not even pausing to acknowledge the strangely worded slur she had just put out into the world.

"You were the one who insisted on a year long contract," I reminded her, then quickly hustled out the door before she could delve any further into the point.

The crazy old bitch had insisted that I sign a year long contract when my friend Emily had insisted I should hire her, which though a bit strange for such things did have the benefit of locking in her compensation for the year, which she only later discovered was well under standard market rates.

Back in the outside world and craving some brunch, though we were getting toward the time of day where it would likely be better called linner or maybe dunch, I went down to D'Angelo's to enjoy some chorizo and eggs rancheros and supposedly bottomless mimosas. Though of course there is a bottom, us all living in a capitalist society and all. D'Angelo's was by far the best place for brunch in the neighborhood, even if oftentimes at least one of the big front windows was covered with plywood due to someone throwing a rock through it. The owners always claimed it was anarchist kids, but those of us in the know knew it was actually the gruff old meat packing locals who used to come to D'Angelo's before the gentrification of the area, back when it was a seedy bar with painted over windows, cheap watered down drinks, and sweepstakes machines. The drinks were no longer cheap, but they were still watered down, and the sweepstakes machines were still there.

In any case, there I was enjoying my third flute and some video clips on my phone, when who should walk in but Greg Gabaldon himself. And not only that, he got all sorts of excited when he saw me and rushed forward like a man on a mission.

I should probably stop to mention that Greg Gabaldon is the gayest looking straight man I've ever met in my life, at least outside of Europe. He was always dressed to the nines, his hair perfectly coiffed. Today he was wearing a slim cut blazer with a calico cat colored scarf loosely wrapped around his neck.

"Damn, I'm glad to see you," he announced in that over the top Greg Gabaldon way of his.

This took me aback a bit, given I don't think Greg Gabaldon had ever been glad to see me a day in either of our lives.

"Hello Greg."

I kept my voice cool so I would seem like the more reasonable one. My secret goal in all of our interactions.

"This is a bit of luck running into you," he said, sitting down in the chair across from me.

It kind of pissed me off, him just sitting down without asking, but he looked fairly stressed out so I decided just to go with it given the unusual nature of the whole situation, never mind the events of this morning.

"I need you to start running the lines for Captain Hook ASAP," he said.

I sighed at the usual Greg Gabaldon bullshit.

"I told you Greg. I'm not going to break my back when we all know I'm just going to be stuck doing Background Pirate #5."

Greg snapped his fingers in my face, a bad habit that made me want to bite one off. Probably his middle finger. It's hard not to notice a missing middle finger.

"You're not getting it," insisted Greg, smacking the table lightly with one hand that way he does when he gets antsy. "You're going to play Captain Hook."

I swear I nearly spit out my mimosa mid-drink like I was in a cartoon or something. I couldn't believe it was actually happening. I couldn't believe it had actually worked.

"What about Mindy?"

Greg dramatically threw his hands into the air.

"Some guy whacked her knee in with a pipe and rode away on a dirt bike. She's going to be out of commission for months."

"A Nancy Kerrigan!" I exclaimed.

To be honest, I was a little let down by the lack of pizzazz on the part of the Devil. One expects a little more conniving creativity. But who was I to complain? I had gotten exactly what I had always wanted. Greg was still talking. Fricking Greg. But I won't bore you with the details. Mindy Gabaldon was out, I was in, and that's what was important. Besides, he left soon after, evidently wanting to get back to his sister in the hospital or something, but I was literally on cloud nine as I nearly skipped with joy back to my apartment.

Part 3 - La Governante

When I got back a big crowd had gathered on the sidewalk in front of my building. The usual mix of hipsters and neo-douches who frequent such areas and have the time to stand around and gawk. Many had their phones out, flashing pictures and recording video. For a conceited, delusional moment I thought they were all there to congratulate me, soon to be the greatest Captain Hook to have ever graced the local repertory theater stage. But of course I was being ridiculous. Nobody was even looking at me. No, they were looking up at the balcony of my third floor apartment where Agatha Christie was yelling down and gesticulating with a fervor, jutting out their nearly non-existent chin as far as it could go. They were roaring down at the crowd, slashing the air with their bony hands like a mad conductor keeping their words in time. Apparently they had just hit the big crescendo.

"Il Duce ha sempre ragione!" they were chanting. "Il Duce ha sempre ragione!"[1]

------

[1] The Leader is always right!

The crowd below was laughing and hooting at them. The damn dingbat had lost their fricking mind. I rushed upstairs to get them off the balcony. I was already on thin ice with the super and I was pretty sure an insane English woman screaming from my apartment wasn't going to help. I rushed up the stairs, foregoing the elevator in a sudden fit of athletic panic, and fumbled with my keys, stabbing at the lock. Finally getting the damn thing in, rarely a problem for me, winky face, I rushed inside and promptly bashed my knee on the credenza, knocking an empty pint bottle to the floor. I stood for a moment, staring at it. It looked vintage. The label was worn nearly off. It was Jose Cuervo. Agatha Christie was still chanting outside.

"That old bitch!" I exclaimed.

Evidently, Agatha Christie had been taking nips from my liquor collection.

Well, if you can't figure out what happened, I'm not going to tell you, given how perfectly obvious it should be to anyone. Agatha Christie decided to have a little drink, choosing a bottle in the back figuring I would be less likely to notice. And then there you go, Benito Mussolini's soul in the body of my housekeeper. Pretty standard stuff, you know.

Not really sure what else to do, I bodily dragged Agatha Christie off the balcony, which wasn't hard given, soul of Mussolini or no, they were still just a frail old lady.

"Toglimi le mani di dosso, comunista. Non sai chi sono?"[2] they bellowed as I dragged them inside.

I had no idea what they were saying, given I don't know any fricking Italian. And even if I did, it would've been hard as hell to understand given they were speaking it with her thick English accent.

"Sit down," I yelled as I hauled them onto the couch.

---

[2] Get your hands off me, communist. Don't you know who I am?

It was a mid-century modern from a dentist's office that closed. Teddy had hooked me up with it as well. I had no complaints about the couch.

"Nessuno mi dice cosa fare, bastardo dal cazzo moscio,"[3] they declared, trying to rise back up, slamming her shoe down onto the faux hardwood floor.

"Sit the frick down," I ordered, shoving them back down. Probably harder than I needed to, but I was in a bit of a panic and it seemed to work.

My downstairs neighbor banged on their ceiling. It didn't worry me. She was a shut in who hated the police in that way that only upper middle class middle aged white women can.

"Corpo da vecchia stupida,"[4] they pouted.

People were still jeering down in the street. I closed the sliding glass door and locked it. Would people be calling the police for elder abuse or something? I mean, they couldn't see into my apartment from the street, but I was definitely on multiple camera phones forcefully dragging what appeared to be a deranged old woman off my balcony.

"Frick," I said.

It wasn't a big apartment, but never before had it ever felt so small.

"Che palle,"[5] asserted Agatha Christie.

"Shut up! Can't you see I'm trying to think?"

"Smettila di perdere tempo! Dobbiamo marciare sul Campidoglio."[6]

The picture of my grandmother on the wall was glowering down at me, though to be fair, it always seemed to be glowering. Gram-Gram was never the most open to the world kind of people.

---

[3] Nobody tells me what to do, you limp-dick bastard.
[4] Stupid old lady body.
[5] What a drag.
[6] Stop wasting time! We must march on the Capitol.

"Please just shut up," I said again, tears nearly in my eyes.

"Hai qualche pistola? Probabilmente avremo bisogno di qualche pistola."[7]

Not knowing what else to do, I turned on the TV and previews for movies and shows started playing. Agatha Christie stared, mouth hanging open.

"Un cinema in questo minuscolo appartamento! Questo è pazzesco."[8]

I walked into the kitchen. There were dirty dishes in the one hole sink. Years of my mother's rules nearly set me to washing them. I had company, even if part of them was supposed to have washed the fricking dishes so I wouldn't have to do it. Instead I grabbed a bag of store brand potato chips went back into the main room.

"Hai film in cui recitano Anita Page o Alida Valli?"[9]

Most of my suggested queue was various Real Housewives knock offs and John Wayne movies. I'm allowed to be a complex person. Don't judge me. I decided on John Wayne. Agatha Christie seemed to enjoy it, at least they quieted down, or maybe she just enjoyed the chips. She most certainly enjoyed the chips. Crumbs got all over the floor and she rubbed her greasy hands on my couch. What in the hell was I supposed to do?

First, I tried calling Teddy. After all, he was the kind of guy who just knew things, but of course he didn't answer and his stupid voicemail was full. I wasn't that surprised. Teddy screened his calls based upon his wants of the day, and though he liked to have me around from time to time, I wasn't always his preferred company.

---

[7] Do you have any guns? We're probably going to need some guns.
[8] A movie theater in this tiny apartment! This is crazy.
[9] Do you have any movies starring Anita Page or Alida Valli?

"You're like Dr. Pepper," he had once explained. "You're awesome when you're wanted, but just the worst if you're not."

Next, I tried searching a bit on my phone, but it's kind of hard to do when you don't know the proper term for something. Possession maybe? There was a lot on demon possession, but that didn't feel right. Two spirit certainly wasn't helpful either, nor was what do you do when an old lady drinks a soul. What little I could wasn't exactly helpful. Most of it being conflicting bullshit undoubtedly made up by people who had never really had the soul of an Italian dictator stuck in their housekeeper.

I had to think. First things first, I had to ascertain if Agatha Christie was even still in their own body. Was that even possible? Was it like being roommates in there or something? Not knowing what else to do, I got down close and stared deep into their eyes.

"Are you in there Annis?" I asked.

Agatha Christie pushed me aside.

"Smettila di oscurare il film con la tua faccia da frociaggine."[10]

I didn't know much Italian, but I definitely knew part of what they said that time. One time when Emily and I had been high and bored we'd looked up homophobic slurs in every language we could think of, and that one had stood out for whatever reason. I'm not sure why. Fate I guess. It didn't make a lot of sense that Benito Mussolini would just know something like that about me, having just met me, which combined with the thick English accent made me feel pretty sure that Agatha Christie and Benito Mussolini were cohabitating.

"I'm going to try to figure this out, Annis," I promised.

---

[10] Stop obscuring the movie with your faggot face.

"Mi hai appena fatto sentire la mancanza del fatto che sparasse a un tizio,"[11] they complained.

I sat down on the other end of the couch and tried to think. Perhaps it was something I could ask the Devil for help with. But if I did, what would he demand in payment? The Devil after all was supposedly a wily bastard, even if apparently not the most creative of sorts. Besides, Teddy had told me he only appears on the crossroads once a month on the night of the full moon. This was definitely something I didn't want to deal with for a month. I mean, did Agatha Christie have a family? I had no idea, but I'm sure somebody would notice if she disappeared for a month.

"Questo cowboy sa davvero sparare,"[12] said Agatha Christie, making finger guns.

Feeling a bit stressed out, I went into the bathroom to take a dispose of the mimosas. I tend to pee more when I'm stressed, and that's when it hit me. Maybe if Agatha Christie drank Benito's soul, they'd eventually pee it out! Why not? If you could drink a soul you should be able to pee out a soul.

I decided to give it a try. After all, what did I have to lose? Coming back out, I went into the kitchen and filled up a big Hydro Flask of water and brought it to Agatha Christie. They did not seem pleased.

"Voglio un frappè al sorbetto alla fragola."[13]

"Drink the water," I insisted, holding it out to them.

"Basta mescolare vino rosso, sorbetto alla fragola e bitter. Quanto è difficile?"[14]

I recognized part of that, something about wine and sorbet, but I didn't like the sound of it. A drunk fascist dictator, even one in an old lady's body, did not sound like

---

[11] You just made me miss him shooting a guy.

[12] This cowboy really knows how to shoot.

[13] I want a strawberry sorbet parfait.

[14] Just mix red wine, strawberry sorbet and bitters. How hard is that?

something I wanted to deal with. But on the other hand, it wasn't like I could just shove a funnel in their mouth.

"If you drink the water I'll get you the wine," I promised.

Agatha Christie nodded their head with a sharp singular motion, took the Hydro Flask of water, and downed it in a single pull. It was pretty impressive, all things considered. They then put the Hydro Flask down on the credenza with a hollow clang and looked at me expectantly. A deal was a deal. I went into the kitchen and poured white wine into the Hydro Flask from the box in my fridge. Agatha Christie took a drink and shuddered.

"Questo non è Mateus, ma immagino che dovrà bastare."[15]

We sat watching the movie. Whenever Agatha Christie ran out of wine, I poured them more. They could drink an impressive amount. The John Wayne movie ended and some other old western started. Agatha Christie pointed to one of the Native Americans on the screen.

"Sono abbastanza sicuro che quel tizio sia italiano."[16]

We were halfway through the new movie when finally, the big moment came. Which was good, given Agatha Christie was beginning to slur a bit and I didn't have much wine left in the box. The old gal must have been quite a drinker.

"Toilette?"[17] they requested with a commanding tone.

"Over there," I pointed.

They got up and waddled over to the bathroom. I must admit, my need to know got the better of me. I went and stood next to the door so I could hear them pee. I swear to God I'm not one of those perverts who pretends to be in line

---

[15] This isn't Mateus, but I guess that will have to do.
[16] I'm pretty sure that guy is Italian.
[17] Do you really need me to translate this one? What are you, some kind of idiot?

at the bathroom just for the sound effects. At first I just heard the toilet seat go up. Then some fumbling around followed by a long silence. Then the toilet seat came back down. You don't need to know the middle part. The toilet flushed. They didn't wash their hands. That's how they caught me. They jerked open the door, catching me standing there.

"Cosa sei, una specie di pervertito del bagno?"[18] they yelled, pushing me out of the way.

I cursed under my breath. Nothing had changed. Agatha Christie, grumbling to themselves, waddled back to the couch, sat down, and finished their Hydro Flask of wine. Then they started to cry.

"Ho conquistato l'Etiopia," they mournfully cried. "Ho conquistato l'Albania."[19]

I wasn't sure what to do.

"Avevo soldati al mio comando. Avevo carri armati. Avevo aeroplani."[20]

They grabbed their chest in a way that looked like it probably hurt.

"Una volta avevo un pene magnifico," they wailed. "Ora ho delle tette da vecchia signora."[21]

What else could I do? I went over and comforted them as best as I could, holding them against me as they drunkenly wept.

"Preferirei morire e tornare all'inferno piuttosto che essere una vecchia signora senza niente," they wailed. "Cosa ho fatto per meritarmi questo?"[22]

---

[18] What are you, some kind of bathroom pervert?

[19] I conquered Ethiopia. I conquered Albania.

[20] I had soldiers under my command. I had tanks. I had airplanes.

[21] I used to have a great penis. Now I have old lady tits.

[22] I'd rather die and go back to hell than be an old lady with nothing. What did I do to deserve this?

They eventually cried themselves out, finally falling asleep after what seemed like an inordinately long amount of time. Carefully extricating myself from them, I began to pace the room, trying to think of what else to do while they snored on the couch.

Benito

Part 4 - Uomo Santo

It wasn't until evening, after I had eaten dinner, a sleeve of Ritz in case you were wondering, when the obvious came to me. An exorcist! I mean, who better to get an extra soul out of somebody? Who better to help with the machinations of the Devil? Unfortunately, this was an area where once again online searching turned up zip in the help department. There was just too much bullshit online to figure out what was true and what was not. About the only thing I got for certain out of my scrolling was the fact that not every Catholic priest was able to do an exorcism.

With that in mind, I finally just said the hell with it and did a map search for exorcising priests in my area. Amazingly enough, this worked. Even more amazingly, one popped up a short bus ride away. Not wanting to lose any time, I shook Agatha Christie awake.

"Sono i partigiani?" they cried as they awakened, their face white with fear. "Sono qui per uccidermi di nuovo?"[23]

It was chilly out and they didn't have a coat so I gave them one of mine. I'm a fairly small person, but it enveloped

---

[23] Are they the partisans? Are they here to kill me again?

their even more slight and droopy frame. We went outside
and stood at the bus stop. When the bus arrived I paid our
fares as we climbed on. There weren't many other people on
the bus.

"Questo autobus puzza di pipì,"[24] they said.

I nodded my head, only half listening. After about
twenty minutes we got off. It was then a couple of blocks of
walking until we arrived at a small but imposing church
made of gray stone. It was built with the walls right up
against the sidewalk, no fronting courtyard or lawn.

"Oh fantastico, la casa dei germi neri,"[25] said Agatha
Christie sarcastically.

"Hush," I hissed.

The main door was locked, so we went to the entrance of
the small rectory next door and I rang the bell. Agatha
Christie was grumbling to themselves, it appearing to be
their favorite hobby. Nothing happened, so I rang the bell
again.

A light came on in a window. A lock rolled back and the
door opened. The man at the door was in the black pants and
short sleeve shirt of a priest, white collar cliched tight around
his neck. He was one of the most imposing men I've ever
seen. I mean seriously, though he wasn't tall, this guy was
built like a brick shithouse dipped in steel, with a boyish
face, a full head of blonde hair, clear blue eyes, and his
muscles bulging as though he was smuggling loafs of bread
under his clothes.

"Ad Adolf sarebbe piaciuto molto questo tizio,"[26] said
Agatha Christie.

"One-o-five and twenty-five," the priest muttered
quietly to himself.

"Hello," I said.

---

[24] This bus smells like pee.
[25] Oh fantastic, the house of the black germs.
[26] Adolf would have really liked this guy.

"Hello," he answered, his voice surprisingly light and sweet. "Can I help you?"

"Puoi bere olio di ricino finché non ti fai la cacca fino alla morte."[27]

The priest looked bemused.

"This is my housekeeper, Agatha... Annis," I tried to explain. "She's having a bit of an issue."

"You can come back tomorrow at eight for confessions," said the priest.

I tried my best to explain, which you probably don't need to hear all about, given you already know. I will say that the priest, whose name turned out to be Father Jim, was a pretty good listener. He nodded at all the right times, asked a couple of questions, and chewed on his lower lip a bit. From the way he acted, you'd think this was all a fairly regular occurrence in his day to day life. When I was done he nodded his head, seemingly deep in thought.

"That's a crazy story," he said.

Agatha Christie had wandered over by the church, where they were cursing and kicking at it with their orthopedic loafer. We both watched until they stopped and walked back over, grumbling.

"What would you like me to do to help?" asked Father Jim.

"I was hoping, I told him, "that maybe you could get Mussolini's soul out with an exorcism."

Father Jim laughed. It was not a cruel laugh, but a light tinkling.

"Oh," he chortled, "this happens all the time. I'm an exercising priest, not an exorcising one."

"Pardon?" I asked.

"Exercising priest. It's something I came up with. I help people find God through rigorous exercise."

---

[27] You can drink castor oil until you poop yourself to death.

"What?" I said, evidently not able to believe what I was hearing.

"The salvation of one's eternal soul are the real gains when you work out with me."

I swear I'm not normally such a crier, but it was all too much to take in. All I had wanted was to play Captain Hook in a stupid play. And now here I was, trying to deal with the supernatural, and failing utterly because of a fricking typo.

"There, there," said Father Jim.

He put a reassuring hand on my shoulder.

"Che bambino,"[28] said Agatha Christie, shaking their head at me.

All of the crying evidently made Father Jim rather uncomfortable. He just stood there, his hand on my shoulder, lips drawn tight, trying to find something else to look at, and then finally letting out a sigh.

"Why don't you come in and we'll see what I can do to help."

"Really?" I asked.

"Sure," said Father Jim.

I hugged him. Good God how I hugged that man. It was like hugging a warm block of iron.

The rectory was filled with exercise equipment. There were barbells, dumbbells, rowing machines, treadmills, and all sorts of other contraptions whose purpose was a mystery given I was naturally blessed with a thin physique that I was perfectly happy not enhancing in a way that required regularly scheduled maintenance. Sorry not sorry. In the corner were a few chairs and a small TV surrounded by stacks of VHS tapes. Who in the hell still has VHS tapes? A mangy looking Jack Russell terrier was sleeping on the weight bench. He raised up and growled when we came in.

---

[28] What a child.

"I also take in stray dogs," explained Father Jim. "That and exercising are my two passions. Well, that and God of course."

He laughed his little tinkling laugh.

"Gli alani sono dei veri cani."[29]

Agatha Christie pursed their lips.

"I leoni sono ancora meglio. Io avevo un leone." Agatha Christie suddenly looked concerned. "Che diavolo è successo al mio leone?"[30]

Father Jim walked over to a fridge and pulled out a plastic water bottle.

"Do you want one?" he asked.

"No thank you," I answered.

"Always good to stay hydrated." He chugged down the whole bottle in a single go. "Plus we'll need the bottle."

"Amavo davvero quel leone,"[31] said Agatha Christie.

"Okee doke," said Father Jim, wiping his mouth with the back of his hand. "You might not want to watch this. It might be pretty gross."

"What do you mean might be?" I asked. "Haven't you done this before?"

Father Jim gave a little shrug.

"It's all right," he said, "I've seen the movie like a dozen times. How hard can it be?"

And with that, he led Agatha Christie into a back room and shut the door behind them. I sat out in the main room with the workout equipment on an old easy chair near the TV and mainly scrolled through my phone and looked over my Captain Hook lines Greg Gabaldon had emailed me. I wasn't really sure what I was supposed to do. A couple of times I tried to pet the little Jack Russell, but he growled at me each

---

[29] Great Danes are real dogs.

[30] Lions are even better. I had a lion. What the hell happened to my lion?

[31] I really loved that lion.

time, showing his little teeth. Then he got up and humped a dumbbell for a bit before lying back down on the bench, which fully convinced me to just leave him alone.

I'm admittedly a bit of a stress sweater. I heaved open a window. It was a nice big leaded window reaching almost to the floor and it let in plenty of nice cool air. It was strangely quiet in the back room. No reciting of prayers, no screaming, nothing that I would have thought would be a part of a proper exorcism. For a bit I put my ear to the door, but all I heard was gagging and unintelligible whispers, which sounded encouraging. Growing bored, I went back to running my lines.

It took close to an hour, but they both finall re-emerged. Father Jim was beaming, a bottle of slightly discolored water in his hand. The sagging woman behind him looked tired.

"Questi maledetti preti," he said, all trace of the thick English accent gone. "Sono ancora bloccato nel corpo di questa stupida vecchia signora."[32]

"What the frick!" I declared.

"All done!" announced Father Jim, sounding very pleased with himself. "It took a bit but we got it out."

"Which one did you get out?" I demanded.

Father Jim looked confused.

"The old English woman of course."

"Why in the hell did you take my housekeeper out of her own body?!"

Father Jim somehow looked even more confused.

"You told me you wanted to get the terrible racist pig out," he said, his soft voice raising a notch.

I was livid.

"Why in the hell would you think that meant the old English lady and not the fascist dictator?" I yelled.

---

[32] These damn priests. I'm still stuck in this stupid old lady's body.

"Mussolini wasn't a racist," Father Jim stated matter of factly.

"What?!" I screamed.

"Questo tizio dovrebbe leggere un libro di storia,"[33] calmy said the spirit of Benito Mussolini in Agatha Christie's body.

"You see, Benito Mussolini didn't think race was really a thing," explained Father Jim in the tone one uses with a child. "He only enacted many policies later because he wanted to be a closer ally with Hitler. You know, as a strategic decision."

"Forse uno dei miei libri. Tutti mi hanno sempre detto che adoravano i miei libri."[34]

I could feel my whole body shaking.

"How in the hell is that better?!" I yelled.

"I didn't say it was better!" yelled back Father Jim. "I didn't say he wasn't a complete asshole!"

I'm not proud of what happened next. I'm not really sure what came over me. I kind of blacked out. All I know is when I came back to my senses I was shaking Father Jim as hard as I could.

"Finalmente qualcuno con le palle,"[35] cheered Benito.

The big priest let go of the water bottle to better fend me off. It was apparently a pretty crappy bottle because the cap popped off the moment it hit the ground. It rolled across the floor, trailing its contents as it went. Father Jim grabbed me around my middle. The Jack Russell started lapping up the water with quick thirsty thrusts of its tongue. Father Jim threw me like a child throwing down their doll. The Jack Russell gave a terrible yelp of pain and terror. I bashed landed against an Arnold Schwarzenegger poster taped to

---

[33] This guy should read a history book.

[34] Maybe one of my books. Everyone always told me they loved my books.

[35] Finally someone with balls.

the wall hard enough that it knocked the wind out of me. The Jack Russell shook itself and then jumped out the open window.

"Oh fuck me!" yelled Father Jim.

"Questo prete parla come una prostituta,"[36] laughed Benito.

"What do you mean oh fuck?" I demanded, picking myself partially up.

"That was your housekeeper's soul in the bottle," Father Jim rattled off in a rush, "but now she's in that dog!"

"Shit!" I yelled.

We both rushed outside, but the dog containing both the soul of a dog and the soul of Agatha Christie was nowhere to be seen.

"You stay here!" I ordered. "I'll try to find that fricking dog!"

"Get some cheese," suggested Father Jim. "He loves cheese."

"What if Agatha Christie doesn't like it?"

"Who's Agatha Christie?"

"My housekeeper!" I yelled.

"I thought her name was Annis," retorted the priest. "Either way it doesn't matter, everyone loves cheese."

"Not the lactose intolerant," I pointed out.

"They like cheese," countered Father Jim. "They just can't eat it."

"Preferisco l'insalata,"[37] said Benito from the open doorway.

Not able to take anymore I took off into the night, a frantic man on a mission.

---

[36] This priest speaks like a prostitute.
[37] I prefer salad.

Part 5 - Cane Randagio

My first stop was a convenience store on the corner to grab a cheese stick. I was so flustered I had trouble making the right payment, so finally I just handed the teenager behind the counter an Alexander Hamilton and left without my change.

Up and down the street I ran, yelling Annis over and over. I was in a panic. When I saw people, I ran up to them. Some ran away. Others stood their ground. Several I actually shook, demanding to know whether or not they had seen a Jack Russell running loose. Most hadn't. Some had. All told me with their eyes wide with wild trepidation matching my own. Several pushed me away. One man tried to punch me, but I was too quick for him. It didn't matter what happened to me, my hysteria was undiminished. There was nothing to me but the need to find Agatha Christie. It had become my everything.

"Have you seen them?!" I screamed at an old woman as I grabbed her coat.

"Fuck off!" she yelled as she slapped me in the face and indignantly marched off.

For being a seasoned citizen she packed quite a wallop, a much harder slap than I expected from an old broad. Down onto the sidewalk I rolled, coming to a halt on my back, nursing a stinging cheek and tender nose.

Turning my head, I spied a Jack Russell half a block away, chewing through a garbage bag to get the delicious leavings within. I scrambled to my feet and rushed forward, then stopped, uncertain. Was it Agatha Christie? It looked like the right dog, but how could I be sure?

I started a slow and cautious approach. I pulled the string cheese out of my pocket and started slowly peeling down the plastic wrapped, trying to make my movements seem chill and non-threatening. The dog looked at me warily, quivering, and poised to bolt.

"Annis," I whispered, holding out the cheese in front of me.

I took another tentative step forward. The dog growled. I was fairly certain I had the right dog.

"Annis," I implored again, doing everything to keep my voice calm, even playful.

The dog eyed me up and down. They took a couple of steps backward then paused.

"Please Annis," I begged.

The dog started panting. Drool dripped to the sidewalk. I took a step forward. The dog stopped panting and took two steps back.

"I'll raise your rate," I promised.

The dog barked.

"I'll double it," I promised.

The dog barked again and happily jogged over to me, jumping into my arms. I was nearly crying again as I fed Agatha Christie the cheese. It was going to be okay. It was all going to be okay.

"What the hell are you doing in my neck of the woods?" asked a voice behind me.

It was Emily. We weren't far from her apartment, a fact that had completely skipped my mind in all the excitement.

"Did your crazy ass get a dog?" she asked, walking up to us with her slightly gapped two front teeth grin.

"Kind of."

Agatha Christie growled.

"Friendly little shit," she said sarcastically, adjusting the bra she wearing as a top under her opened puffy jacket.

"They grow on you," I promised.

"Is she a boy or a girl?"

I wasn't quite sure what the correct nomenclature would be, given the situation.

"Don't gender my dog!" I blurted, undoubtedly more forcefully than was needed, but I was feeling fricking stressed out.

"Looks like two bitches to me," laughed Emily. She was the only one I still let call me a bitch. "Just like that bitch housekeeper I used to have."

Emily leaned in closer, narrowing her gaze. Emily has widely spaced eyes that kind of bulge, which combined with her snub nose gives her a bit of a Boston Terrier look. Agatha Christie growled louder. They were literally shaking in my arms.

"She even kind of reminds me of her," said Emily.

"Used to have?" I stupidly asked.

"Oh yeah. I caught her stealing some of my liquor. I fired her on the spot because I don't put up with shit from nobody."

She snapped her fingers three times in a triangular motion when she said the last bit. Agatha Christie was straining forward, wiggling themselves free.

"Bitch didn't even do a good job," declared Emily.

Agatha Christie burst forward, liberating themselves from my arms.

"Frick!" I yelled.

"Fuck!" yelled Emily, clutching her arm where Agatha Christie had bit her.

Blood was flowing between her fingers. Agatha Christie fell to the street.

"Your fucking dog bit me!"

Agatha Christie made a run for it.

"Frick!" I yelled again as I started after the little form dashing away.

"Didn't you hear me?! It's really fucking bad!"

Maybe she said other things. I don't know. I was too busy giving chase. Down the block, around a corner. We hit a busy street, two lanes on either side. Agatha Christie made a dash for it. A car screeched to a halt. I ran full tilt into it, inadvertently throwing myself across its hood. The other three lanes didn't stop. Agatha Christie dived. Agatha Christie dodged. Agatha Christie somehow made it to the other side. I painfully rolled off the hood. The woman driving screamed some not very creative curses at me and sped away. The cars wouldn't stop. I had to run two blocks to the nearest crosswalk and wait impatiently for the what must have been the longest light in the world to change. When I got to the other side of the street where I had last seen them, it was too late. They were gone.

With nothing to show for my efforts, I dejectedly made my way back to the rectory. I supposed I should have checked on Emily. She'd already left me multiple irate texts, but I just didn't have the energy to do anything but sulk. When I got back to the rectory, Father Jim and Benito were playing Monopoly. Benito was studying the board, stroking his nearly non-existent chin. Father Jim shrugged his broad shoulders.

"She saw it on the shelf and wanted to play."

38

"Il segreto è controllare le ferrovie,"[38] muttered Benito.

"She cheats," stated Father Jim.

"Questo gigantesco topo nero voleva essere l'auto. Sono sempre l'auto."[39]

"Do you understand what he's saying?" I asked.

Father Jim looked confused.

"Why would I know what she's saying?"

"Doesn't the Pope know Italian?"

"Il papa era la mia piccola puttanella,"[40] muttered Benito.

"Do I look like the Pope?" asked Father Jim in a condescending tone just barely detectable underneath his sweet timbre. "Am I wearing a big tall hat?"

"Ho sempre desiderato indossare quel gigantesco cappello da papa,"[41] mumbled Benito.

Benito rolled the dice. He moved the car onto Ventnor Avenue, which had three houses on it.

"Porca miseria!"[42] screamed Benito, swiping the board off the table with his flabby old arm.

"So how'd it go?" asked Father Jim.

I almost snapped something along the lines of how do you think, do you see a damn dog, but I didn't. Instead, I just explained what had happened. To give credit where credit is due, Father Jim was definitely a good listener. Just like before he nodded at the right times and asked the right questions at the right moments. The guy is a real pro. When I was done he just sat in his chair, obviously deep in thought.

"We have to find that dog," he stated.

I stifled down the urge to say no doy or something else along those lines.

---

[38] The secret is to control the railways.
[39] This giant black mouse wanted to be the car. I'm always the car.
[40] The Pope was my little whore.
[41] I've always wanted to wear that giant pope hat.
[42] Pig misery!

"No shit Sherlock," I said.

I don't always have good self-control when it comes to such things, and he was beginning to try my patience. Father Jim cracked his knuckles. It sounded like he smashing bubble wrap, the kind with the big bubbles.

"Couldn't we just put Mussolini back into an empty bottle so we don't have him wandering around?" I asked.

Father Jim shook his head.

"No good. An empty body just standing around is going to get filled by any old spirit floating around. God only knows who or what we might end up with."

"Really?"

"Fantasmi di sperma," muttered Benito. "Fantasmi di sperma ovunque."[43]

Father Jim nodded, looking past me at a wall covered in motivational workout posters and a fairly nice crucifix with an Asian Jesus on it.

"Oh yeah," he said, "that's Seminary 101."

"What are we going to do?"

Father Jim did a couple of isometric exercises with his arms and then went still again.

"I could probably call Rhonda," he said with a shrug. "She works down at animal control."

"Is she reliable?"

"She can bench one-eighty-five."

It was getting pretty late. Father Jim promised to call Rhonda in the morning and let me know as soon as he heard anything. We exchanged phone numbers. To my complete delight, he also promised to keep Benito at the rectory.

"Prima perdo il pene, ora devo vivere con questo topo nero," complained Benito. "Figlio di puttana."[44]

---

[43] Sperm ghosts. Sperm ghosts everywhere.

[44] First I lose my penis, now I have to live with this black rat. Son of a bitch.

"I'm basically here except for morning mass every day," he explained, "and seven days of mass never hurt anyone."

By the sour look on Benito's old lady face, he didn't agree, but I didn't argue. Father Jim was doing me a solid. I got back on the bus, went home, and went to sleep praying that they'd find Agatha Christie soon.

Benito

Part 6 - Sporco Harry

The next morning I did the usual things you're supposed to do when you lose a dog. I called vet offices, posted on various lost pet social media groups, put even more posts on various missing pet websites, and even printed out posters and hung them up all around the neighborhood where they had last been seen. I didn't have a picture of canine Agatha Christie, so I just found a generic picture of a Jack Russell online that looked close enough.

In the afternoon I went to rehearsal, which was so delicious I almost gagged taking it all in. Mindy Gabaldon was in the front row, with pretty much her whole leg in a cast that was propped up on a metal chair, glaring at me as though she wished she could make me disintegrate with nothing but her dirty looks. It was fricking amazing. Too bad Mindy. Maybe if you hadn't been such a prima donna bitch all the time, things would have turned out better for you.

Greg Gabaldon gave a lot of smiles whenever he gave me direction, which apparently he thought had to be a lot. This would have annoyed the crap out of me if it wasn't for

the fact that this close to opening, we both knew he didn't
have any other options. Which was probably why his smiles
looked so wonderfully forced. Too bad Greg, maybe next time
don't give your fricking sister all the best parts.

I wasn't sure how the rest of the cast felt about my
elevation. They're all professionals, but you know what?
Screw them too, I'm sure for one reason or another. It was
my fricking time to shine.

That night I tried to text Emily a few times to see how
she was doing, but she didn't text back. She was never one to
let things go. She still has a grudge against a boyfriend she
cheated on ten years ago because she insists he forced her
into it. It's a weird story and not mine to tell. I didn't feel all
that bad. I mean, sorry our once mutual housekeeper now
trapped in the body of a dog bit the crap out of you because
you were badmouthing them. Sometimes that's just the
breaks. It's nothing to hold a grudge about.

I was so utterly exhausted from looking for Agatha
Christie all morning and basking in my victorious ascension
all afternoon that I fell asleep without calling Father Jim.

The next day was much like the first. Checking lost dog
forums, printing out and hanging up more posters, and then
rehearsal in the afternoon. I didn't bother texting Emily
again, but I sure as hell called Father Jim.

"Hello," said the priest when he picked up the phone.

I could hear a movie playing in the background.

"Do I feel loocky?" I heard Benito say on the other end
in a sharp barking old lady voice. "Well do I poonk?"

"Quiet please," I heard Father Jim say.

"Anything new?" I asked.

"Who is this?"

I could feel my teeth grind together.

"Who do you think this is?" I huffed.

"Oops, sorry," said Father Jim, "I forgot to put your
number in my phone."

I could feel one of my eyes twitch a little bit.

"How are things going over there?"

"Just fine! Benito is really thriving. She can bench thirty-five."

I wasn't sure I had heard correctly.

"You had him lifting weights?"

"Oh yeah," responded Father Jim. "She seemed a bit down so I thought it would cheer her up a bit."

It sounded like Benito was making impressively accurate gunshot sounds with his mouth.

"Quiet please," I heard Father Jim say again.

"What do you mean, down?" I asked, putting an emphasis on the last word.

"Well, yesterday she tried to kill herself twice," explained Father Jim, "but it's okay, she's not very good at it."

My left eye was definitely twitching.

"He's not very good at it?"

"Well obviously," replied Father Jim with a bit of a patronizing tone. "First she tried to drop a plugged in toaster in the bathtub. Then she tried sticking her head in the oven."

I was gripping my phone so hard my knuckles were starting to hurt.

"He stuck his head in the oven?" I dumbly repeated.

"Oh yeah," Father Jim replied. "But it's not even gas. It's electric."

The sound of gunshots resounded over the phone again. I involuntarily flinched.

"Turn it down please," I heard Father Jim say before returning to me. "I don't even think you can kill yourself that way with modern gas stoves. She really doesn't seem to have much of a grasp on modern technology."

I took the phone away from my head and took a deep breath. When I put it back to my ear I realized Father Jim was still talking.

"...into movies," he said. "She really seems to like Dirty Harry. It's really been helping her English..."

"Look..." I tried to interrupt.

"Or maybe it's re-learning? I don't know much about Mussolini," continued Father Jim. "I tried to read up on him yesterday, but I'm not much of a reader and all of the audio book narrators had really boring voices."

I nearly threw my phone to the floor.

"What about that whole not a racist factoid that got us into this mess?!" I yelled.

The other end of the phone was silent except for the TV. Maybe it was a bit dramatic, but I am an actor after all.

"Goo ahead, mak ma day!" I heard Benito bellow.

"That's not the right part of the movie," I heard Father Jim say. Then he returned to me. "That's pretty much the only Mussolini factoid I know. I think it was on one of those old listicle websites."

I let out a silent scream and got myself back under control.

"I know it's stressful, but maybe you should relax a bit," suggested the priest. "Try praying. That's always good. Or work on your biceps, triceps, shoulders, and traps. That always helps me."

I took a couple of deep breaths.

"Okay," I said, keeping my voice as even as I could. "Has your friend at animal control heard anything about Agatha Christie yet?"

"Who?" asked Father Jim.

"The. Dog. With. My. Housekeeper's. Soul. In. It!"

I spit out each word between clenched teeth.

"Oh, you mean Peaches," replied Father Jim. "The dog's name is Peaches, or at least that's what I called him when he was here. Not really sure why. He just seemed like a Peaches."

"Here es a seven point sooppository!" yelled Benito.

"Wrong movie," I heard Father Jim say.

I hung up the phone. I just couldn't take any more of the conversation.

The next day was pretty a repeat of the other two, except I was beginning to grow a little worried that we were never going to find Agatha Christie. While I was on my way to practice Father Jim texted me to let me know his friend Rhonda at animal control hadn't heard anything yet. And that that Benito had gotten up to forty on the bench press. I was so distracted I wasn't really able to enjoy the glares of Mindy Gabaldon, which hadn't diminished a bit, and grew especially virulent since I kept flubbing my lines.

"How hard is it to say I'm the nautical knave of Neverland," she demanded, pounding the arms of her seat with frustration while her brother gnawed on his upper lip and sweated through his shirt.

That evening, I treated myself and stopped to pick up some shrimp pad-thai. I was starting to mull over what it would be like if we didn't find Agatha Christie. I mean, if you really think about it, the result would just be Benito Mussolini being alive for another ten to fifteen years in an old lady's body and Agatha Christie getting to live as a dog. Neither of which seemed all that bad. Think about it. Who hasn't wished at some point they could be a dog? And as far as Benito went, well screw that guy.

I was so deep in these thoughts that I didn't that there were two men waiting for me outside my apartment until I nearly walked right into them. Large bulky men in old worn pea coats and matching porkpie hats. The less heavy set of the two had bloodshot eyes and a five o'clock shadow. The bigger one was clean shaven and had deep set piggish eyes in a face that looked like a lump of bread dough.

"Scuse me," said the less heavy set of the two in a rough English accent that sounded a bit put on. "I was wonderin if I could take a moment of yer time."

"I'm pretty busy," I said, wondering if these two were the roughest looking Jehovah Witnesses I had ever seen.

"My name es Nigel," said the less heavy set man. "And this es my associate, The Grip."

The Grip smiled, revealing a mouth completely full of golden teeth.

"We're lookin fer Annis Lancaster," said Nigel.

A cold sweat slipped across my brow and another down my back.

"Who?" I asked, my voice giving off a little prepubescent squeak.

"Yer housekeeper," explained Nigel in a tone that was both calm and menacing. "Blimey," he said, glancing back at The Grip, "this bloody bitch doesn even know the name of their own housekeeper."

The Grip gave out a snicker that sounded like released high pressure steam. He was looking at me like I was some kind of tasty morsel he could just pop into his mouth, grind up with his golden teeth, and swallow down, bones and all.

"Oh, that Annis," I answered, doing my best to sound sure but yet uncertain. "I haven't seen her since she cleaned my apartment a few days ago."

Nigel nodded his big head.

"Es that so, es that so," he said. "Well, ere's the thing, chapette, yours was the last place she cleaned before she seemingly disappeared, and her niece's boyfriend is gettin quite concerned. Quite concerned indeed."

I didn't like chapette, but I don't like lots of things people call me. I try not to let such things bother me.

"Her niece isn't worried?" I asked instead, almost instantly wishing my mouth wasn't always on automatic, yearning for the ability to suck the words back up into my dumbass maw.

The Grip did his hissing laugh again. Nigel clucked his tongue like a disapproving matron.

"Ere now, ere now," he said, smiling in the most unfriendly manner. "The bloody interpersonal foibles of our employer es really none of either of ours concern, es they?"

For a moment I thought he was going to put an arm around my shoulder like we were old confidantes, but he didn't do any more than lean in closer.

"What es the concern of all present company es the current location of our mutual good friend, Annis Lancaster."

"I told you," I said, managing to keep my voice steadier the second time around. "I haven't seen her since she cleaned my apartment."

"Okay, okay," said Nigel, still smiling. "But if ya do see er of course you'll let us know?"

It sounded like a question, but it sure as hell didn't feel like a question. Nigel took a step forward so his bulk was practically right on top of me. I nodded my head, unable to squeak out a sound.

"Just don't go nowheres fer a bit," he said menacingly. "I'd hate ta have anyone think ya were involved en anything untoward and running away or somethin."

His breath stank of curry and some kind of heavy malty beer. He shoulder checked me as he moved past. The Grip stood staring at me for a moment more, smiling at me with his golden teeth. Then he smacked the container of shrimp pad-thai out of my hands and ground it into the sidewalk under his feet.

"Chucky's clodhoppers," grunted Nigel. "Why'd ya do that fer? Now ta whole damn car es going to stink like bloody shrimp and tamarind ya wanker."

The Grip just shrugged his large doughy shoulders.

"Bloody ell," said Nigel, "King Stephen's brass bum."

The pair walked down the street. I waited until they were out of sight then went upstairs to pack myself a change of clothes, my toothbrush, and my syringes. Grabbing my phone charger from the bedroom, I hightailed it out of there on the next bus towards Father Jim's church and rectory.

Part 7 - Il Duce è Triste

I won't bore you with the details of my time staying at
the rectory. Let's just say that it was a lot of dealing with a
very nonchalant and sweaty priest, playing far too many
games of Monopoly, and watching Dirty Harry movies over
and over again. Did you know that there are five Dirty
Harry movies? I sure as hell didn't, but I sure the frick did
after a single day at the rectory.

I'm not ashamed to admit I was scared shitless. I didn't
go home. I didn't go to rehearsals. I didn't even leave the
rectory. I was a real mess. There was no way in hell Nigel
and The Grip wouldn't do terrible things to me if Agatha
Christie didn't pop up soon. Maybe even still if she did. I
knew this because Nigel somehow found my phone number
and left me a wonderfully descriptive series of voicemails
from a blocked number. That's right, voicemail. Who the
hell is still leaving voicemails?

"Look ere ma little candy cane," he said in a syrupy
voice. "All we want ta know es what's appened to Annis
Lancaster, that's all. Nothin big. We just know that ya know
more than yer lettin on and it's makin our employer

decidedly unhappy. We've noticed ya aven't been ome much of late or at yer little play rehearsals. Some people might say that yer acting a bit suspicious. Perhaps ya can meet us outside yer apartment tomorrow to talk about it."

The one a few days later was more to the point.

"We know ya know somethin ma little dewdrop," he said, his voice several octaves lower this time. "Ma associate is oping we have ta figure this out the ard way."

I could hear The Grip snickering in the background.

"But I'm more of an even tempered fella. Ya need to meet us outside yer ouse tomorra mornin."

The last one a few days after that skipped over all pretense.

"We're goin ta find ya, ma pretty, and we're goin to urt ya."

Greg Gabaldon also texted me constantly, each iteration becoming more desperate than the last, until they broke over into pure and unbridled fury, followed by another bout of begging, and then fury once again, and finally telling me that he was going in a different direction for the play and that I could forget even being Background Pirate #5. I didn't bother to text back. In comparison to two brutes beating the ever living crap out of me it didn't seem all that important.

Emily also texted me, calling me a shit eating donkey for letting my dog bite her and then caring more about the dog than her. I almost texted her back given I felt this was a pretty high horse to be on for someone who had once falsely told a waiter her mother had died just to get a free basket of fries, but in the end I never hit send. I was having enough drama in my life without adding to it needlessly.

For my part, I tried to text and call Teddy, but of course still received no answer.

"Dr. Pepper has twenty-three flavors," he once told me. "Sometimes that's just too many damn flavors."

As for Father Jim, aside from his religious duties the man pretty much spent the entire time exercising. Well, that and once a day eating a thin sliver of cake. He had a whole sheet cake in the fridge that he must have gotten on discount given that the Happy Birthday message was to somebody named Liam and one of the P's in Happy was missing. He really drew out eating each sliver, little nibble after little nibble, a look of complete gratification on his face the whole time. He of course offered me some, but I always declined, politely at first, but then more forcefully as the week went on. He also offered some to Benito, who unlike me, was more than happy to indulge to his heart's content, often times even when it wasn't being offered.

Father Jim also suggested on multiple occasions that I try doing some praying or sit ups, or maybe both together.

"It cleanses the troubled soul," he promised.

Much like the cake, at first I politely declined, but then as the days wore on I got more nasty about it until finally he pretty much left me alone entirely. Which didn't feel great, but did feel better than being pestered all the time. In this way Benito was a much better rectorymate. He largely ignored me, only occasionally voicing an opinion directed at me, not all of them sensical.

"You know what makes me really sick to my stoomach?" he'd say. "Watching you stuff your face with those hot dogs!"

While I was rather impressed with how quickly he had eradicated any trace of an accent, his skills were seemingly more in line with a parrot than some kind of language savant. I wasn't even eating hot dogs. It's from the fourth Dirty Harry movie. I cannot minimize how many times I watched those fricking movies. They run through my skull constantly now. Fuck Benito Mussolini.

I guess one thing worth mentioning is that Benito did try to kill himself two more times while I was there. Both times with knives from the kitchen, but Father Jim and I stopped him before he could even put a scratch on Agatha Christie's body. After the second time, Father Jim took all of the knives and locked them away in the tabernacle in the church. Benito frantically cried when he did it.

"Perché non mi lasci semplicemente morire?"[45] he wailed, pounding his old tits with his hands.

Despite the language barrier, Father Jim seemed to get the gist of what was being said.

"Because it's not your body," he explained. "We have to get the old lady back into her body."

"Questa vecchia signora ha l'intestino allentato e la sciatica."[46]

"Plus it's a mortal sin. And things could always be worse."

Benito just sneered and guffawed as though Father Jim didn't know what he was talking about.

"It's true," insisted the priest, "You should see what happened to your old pal Hitler."

Benito paled and quickly waddled from the kitchen back to his chair in front of the TV, still sobbing.

"Is that true?" I asked.

Father Jim shrugged.

"How should I know?"

Father Jim seemed to be full of assumptions regarding things he didn't really know about.

"You think he'd rather be alive as an old woman than dead," I later mused.

"Machismo is a big thing in Italy," replied Father Jim, sweating his way through some deadlifts. "Even in the clergy. Why do you think they won't let women be priests or bishops? Too many Italians in charge."

I looked at him, trying to gauge if he was being serious.

---

[45] Why don't you just let me die?
[46] This old lady has loose bowels and sciatica.

"What about Pope Joan?"

Father Jim just shrugged, which was fairly impressive
for a man with a barbell hovering above his head.

"Even if it was true, I don't think being tied to a horse's
tail by the feet and dragged to death while people throw
rocks at you counters the whole machismo thing."

I had to admit, he probably had a point. In the chair in
front of the TV, Benito was still sulking, his hands on his
chest, lifting and dropping the old tits underneath his shirt.

"Or maybe he just wishes he had better knockers," I
suggested.

The priest let the barbell fall to the concrete floor with a
loud bang and just shrugged again. The man certainly
shrugged a lot.

Animal Control Rhonda didn't call for an entire
week. By that time, I was barely speaking at all to either of
my rectorymates. When Father Jim answered his phone and
said the name Rhonda, I started watching him like a hawk,
trying to discern the words from the other side through pure
force of will. Benito kept watching his movies. Father Jim
made small talk. He joked. He laughed. He gave exercise
tips. Finally, after far too long he hung up the phone.

"Well?" I asked, unable to contain myself.

"Peaches got caught by animal control."

"Excellent!"

I was overfilled with delight.

"Five days ago," Father Jim added. "Peaches got caught
by animal control five days ago and since he wasn't chipped
or licensed they put him on a truck to a pet adoption agency
in New York City."

I stood there, my mouth hanging open.

"I guess there's more soft hearted people in the Big
Apple than in the Midwest," he added.

I wanted to shake the bulky figure in front of me, but
that lesson had already been learned the hard way. My

mouth moved a bit. At first no sound emerged, but then the words began to squeak out.

"I thought you said she was reliable," I said with barely contained restraint.

Father Jim's face was the face of a simpleton. He shrugged his ridiculously broad shoulders. Was that his fricking answer to fricking everything?

"I thought she was. Though come to think of it, I've never actually seen her bench one-eighty-five. That's just what she told me."

"Nothing wrong with shooting," declared Benito, pointing finger guns at the TV screen, "as long as the right people get shot."

Father Jim chuckled a bit.

"What in the frick are we supposed to do now?" I asked.

Father Jim shrugged.

"Go to New York City I guess."

The man was pissing me off to no end. But in this I had to admit, he once again had a good point.

Part 8 - Tutti a Bordo

Early the next morning all three of us hustled to the train station. Father Jim had insisted he and Benito come along.

"We'll just do it there rather than risk having you try to make it back with Peaches," he had explained in a cheerful upbeat tone. "I've been reading up on exorcisms, so I think I'll have it down this time. The narrators for those audio books are much better."

"What about your parishioners?" I had asked.

"It'll be okay," he had laughed. "I'll just set up a recording and one of them can hit play. The handful of seniors who come won't mind. It's what I do when I go down to Jacksonville every now and again. I'm a huge Jaguars fan."

"Fascinating," I had said dryly, my sarcasm bleeding through.

It was the first time in my life I'd ever been to Grand Central Station. I didn't even know we still had a train station, but you know who doesn't get to fly? Old ladies possessed by Italian fascists, especially ones who don't carry a valid form of identification with them when they clean other people's homes, let alone cash or credit cards. You know who else apparently doesn't have a lot of cash on hand? Priests who use most of the money they collect to help stray dogs and buy workout equipment. I had to put all three tickets on my credit card.

When we got out onto the platform the train was there, but not yet ready to depart, something being wrong with the something or other. I really don't have a lot of knowledge about how trains work. Either way, we were allowed to climb aboard and take our seats.

"Ho fatto in modo che i treni arrivassero in orario,"[47] whined Benito.

"Ah-ah," chided Father Jim. "In English please."

"Feck you."

Father Jim gave Benito a dirty look. Benito just scowled back.

"Dovrei semplicemente buttarmi sotto un treno,"[48] he muttered sullenly.

Father Jim pulled an iPad and some headphones from his messenger bag and got Benito back to watching movies. He was so much easier to handle when watching movies. The train car only had a few people in it. I hopped off to try and find a snack and to take care of some other things.

The station was a big old building with all sorts of little nooks and crannies filled with kiosks, phone charging stations, a couple of old payphones, and other such things. A few of the kiosks looked like they should sell snacks, but all were closed. I found a bathroom first. I hesitated for a moment outside the two entryways like I always do, but of course went into the men's room side. It wasn't very

---

[47] I made sure the trains arrived on time.
[48] I should just throw myself under a train.

big. There were two stalls, both with somebody in them. A man was shaving at the counter. Not really wanting to wait around, I pulled the syringe out of my fanny pack. The shaving man glanced toward me.

"It's medical," I explained, doing my best to smile in a friendly manner while I pulled up the sleeve of my shirt.

"None of my business," answered the man.

I took the cap off the syringe. The man was still watching me.

"Diabetic?" he asked.

"Sure," I said, wincing as I plunged the needle into my arm.

Repacking my fanny pack, I exited and found some vending machines clear back near the entrance with the big old stairs. You know, the stairs from that one movie with that one guy with the shootout and the baby carriage. I bought a little bag of chips and a Dr. Pepper, because that's the only pop they had. I turned to head back when who should I see striding down the stairs? Fricking Nigel.

What the frick was fricking Nigel doing here? For a moment he didn't see me, as I was a bit tucked away by the machines, but he was definitely looking as though he knew I would be there. It made me a bit paranoid, like Emily levels of paranoid. I mean sure, maybe he was looking for someone else, but what were the odds of that?

Feeling it was better to be safe than sorry, I tried to wedge myself in next to the Dr. Pepper machine to hide, but it was no good. There wasn't enough room even for my slim physique. I saw his eyes land on me and his mouth twist into a self-satisfied sneer.

"Oy, there ya are ya flap slapper!" he yelled. "Think ya can skip town, do ya?!"

He started hustling down the stairs as fast as he could. My heart skittered wildly towards a billion beats a minute. I literally thought it was going to explode. Nigel's eyes were narrowed, not in a hostile way, but in the way of a butcher trying to finish up work on time so he can go out and have a few drinks with that cute new bakery girl with the nice cupcakes. I didn't know what to do. I didn't know where to run. So instead I just threw my can of Dr. Pepper at him as hard as I could.

The world slowed down. The maroon can sliced through the air between us, arching upwards on a parabolic trajectory. Nigel saw the can leave my hand. His hang dog eyes widened. His downward descent de-accelerated. The can reached the vertex of its path and began its descent. I'm not sure why so much of my high school mathematics courses came back to me in that moment, but they did. The velocity of the can increased as it began to fall down, down, down toward its target. Nigel's lips opened into an expectant grimace. The can struck with an audible impact like a hard slap, the consensual kind between two bored lovers testing their limits. The seal of the can broke, sending sticky brown prune tasting carbonation spraying across the stairway and the various people ascending and descending. Down dropped the broken can to the floor.

And down went the poor woman standing halfway down the stairs from Nigel.

Blood intermingled with the spilled pop. The woman began to scream, clutching at her head where the can had hit her. Other people began to scream. Nigel stared down at me with a mixed look of surprise and contempt. He spat out something that I could not hear through all the shrieks, but was obviously some kind of curse or oath or other exclamation of that sort.

Down the stairs he came again, skirting the edge of the small but growing crowd around the woman. For a moment my hand instinctively rose to throw my bag of chips as well, but the portion of my brain controlling fight or flight kicked over to the better solution. The chips dropped from my hand as I sprinted as fast as I could back into the cavernous depths of the station.

The rest was all a bit of a blur, but eventually I found myself in front of the dual entryway of an out of the way bathroom. This time around I didn't have time to think. I didn't hesitate. It was purely ingrained habit. Into the ladies room I went, into an empty stall, where I cowered on top of the toilet, my feet up next to my butt, shaking like a fricking altar boy on Palm Sunday.

Okay, so this was my basic plan. I wasn't sure how Nigel had found me, but he had. And most likely that meant The Grip was there as well, the two of them undoubtedly searching for me. I had to get back to the train, but if I left my toilet perch too early they would surely find me. That meant my best option was a last minute escape. Eventually the PA system would announce that train's imminent departure, at which point I would emerge to rush to the platform and escape just in the nick of time, hoping they didn't find Father Jim and Annis in the meantime. It all seemed so simple in my head.

What actually happened was I sat there for a good fifteen minutes, listening to multiple women use the facilities, several of whom should probably change their diets given the sounds and smells they made. Then there was nobody, just the sounds of a tap someone left slightly open so that the constant dripping might drive me half insane. Drip. Drip. Drip. Seriously, who the hell leaves a faucet on like that? Don't they know it wastes water? Don't they know the fricking ice caps are melting?

Somebody came in. Somebody with heavy footfalls.

I held my breath, hoping the drip of the sink would cover the wild, undoubtedly audible, beat of my heart. The somebody started moving down the line of toilets. I sat perfectly still, holding my breath. The somebody started jiggling the doors, seeing if they would pop open. I could hear them breathing. It was raspy. I could imagine the sour face of Nigel or the golden toothed grin of The Grip.

The footfalls and jiggling doors drew closer. Every part of my body itched, demanding to be scratched. A tickle in the back of my throat turned into a sharp twinge, begging me to clear my throat. A shadow appeared under the bathroom door. The door was too low and the angle too sharp to see anything more. The person on the other side let loose a barking cough which echoed around the tiled room. I involuntarily jerked. My elbow hit the metal tampon receptacle attached to the wall. It let out a sharp ding. It hurt like the dickens. I heard a sharp intake of breath.

"Screw you!" I screamed, kicking out with both feet.

The cheap lock on the stall door snapped and out swung the door, slamming into the person on the other side, knocking them to the ground. The door ricocheted back toward me and I kicked it again, catching the person once more, but this time with me following right behind.

"Muffa fucka!" yelled the person on the floor, their voice muffled by blood and a likely broken nose.

It was an older woman wearing a janitor's apron. Blood was pouring from her nose in scarlet ribbons. She was wearing heavy work boots. Her cart was over by the door. I caught my balance on the counter with the sinks.

"I'm so sorry!" I called out to her.

She ripped a walkie talkie out of her pocket.

"Securty to th est bthroom!" she screamed into it, blood still pouring down her face.

"It was an accident!" I frantically yelled.

"I've ben assalted!" screamed the old woman into the walkie talkie.

I ran out of the bathroom. The janitor, seemingly quite spry for her age, was not far behind.

"Securty!" she yelled through her broken nose, pointing at my retreating form. "Securty!"

Everyone was turning to look. Nigel appeared in the direction of the trains, cracking his knuckles when he saw me. I moved to escape the other way, but The Grip appeared, smiling his golden smile like a cat with a cornered mouse. There was nowhere to go. Nothing I could do. Nigel got to me first. He grabbed me roughly by the arm.

"Ya got a lot of bloody..." he snarled.

That's all he managed to get out. The boulder-like fist of Father Jim hit him right in the throat. Suddenly all he could do was gurgle horribly as he dropped to the polished floor, his pork pie hat rolling away as he landed. People started screaming. People in train stations apparently just love to fricking scream. I swear that Emily and I once saw a guy get tased by the TSA at the airport and nobody batted an eye, but here everyone was ready to go full soprano at the drop of a hat.

"One-ninety-five!" yelled Father Jim.

"What?!" I yelled back.

"C'mon!"

He grabbed me by the arm and dragged me with him. We ran back toward the platform.

"All aboard!" hollered one of the station employees, either oblivious to the chaos behind us or not caring about anything beyond railway timetables.

We were nearly to our car, but The Grip had already reached the platform. For a bulky boy he was amazingly quick. We frantically hauled ourselves up the train steps into the car. The conductor insisted on seeing our already hole punched tickets. The Grip was sprinting down the length of the platform, running past our window to get to the nearest door. He grinned malevolently at us. The smile of a man who greatly enjoyed his work.

"Two-twenty," murmured Father Jim.

The Grip's beady eyes fell on Benito through the glass, sitting calmly and watching his iPad, shielded by his headphones from the chaos erupting around him. The Grip pulled up short. He looked perplexed, his head turned to the side like a puzzled dog.

Father Jim jumped off the train, pushing his way past the conductor, and punched The Grip, once straight into the bulging gut, doubling him over, and then an uppercut into his face. The Grip went down. Benito was watching the whole thing.

"This is a .44 Magnum," Benito declared. "The most powerful handgun in the world and will blow your head clean off."

Benito had a shit eating grin on his face. His cheeks were flushed. There was a glint in his eye which made me uncomfortable.

Father Jim climbed back onto the train. The conductor didn't even try to stop him.

"All aboard!"

The conductor pulled the door closed and made his way forward into the next car. The few other people in our car were all looking at their phones, completely shut away from the outside world. The Grip lay wheezing on the ground. He rose up onto his elbow, his eyes two cold black pieces of flint. He spit something onto the platform. Benito waved at him cheerfully. The Grip didn't try to rise any further. The train began to move. We pulled away from the platform, away from The Grip, and out of the station.

Part 9 – In Transito

The train picked up speed, out into the back end of ruined industrial districts and crumbling suburbs. Father Jim was still standing by the door, his boyish face pale.

"I'm going to have to do at least one hundred Hail Mary's and two hundred pushups to make up for that one," he sighed.

Benito laughed.

"When a naked man is chasing a woman through an alley with a butcher's knife and a hard-on," he hollered, "I figure he isn't out collecting for the Red Cross!"

A couple of people in the car looked up from their phones at that one, but still nobody gave it too much mind. Old ladies were funny, but not funny enough to give more than a few seconds of precious attention.

"Shut up," I ordered, my voice perhaps just a bit too abrasive.

"Calm down," advised Father Jim in a soothing voice, walking down the aisle toward us.

"Screw off," I shot back.

Father Jim took in a deep breath through his nose and let it out through his mouth.

"I'm guessing those are the two guys who came to your house," he said, rubbing his bulbous knuckles.

I nodded. My heart was still going a like a drum at a grindcore show. Father Jim seemed to consider my answer for a moment, then dropped to the floor and started doing pushups, rapidly reciting Hail Mary's as he pumped up and down. Several peoples' eyes drifted from their phones, watching him. Apparently an exercising priest on a train was more interesting than a foul mouthed old lady.

"What in the hell do you think you're doing?" I demanded.

"Absolving myself of my sins," he answered without looking up.

"How many of those did you do when you screwed up the exorcism?"

"Enough."

"We wouldn't be here if you hadn't screwed up."

"We wouldn't be here if you hadn't made a deal with the Devil."

That shut me up pretty good. I sat in silence, listening to the rhythmic grunts of Father Jim doing his version of a modern day flailing. A few of the passengers pointed their phones his way to record or take pictures.

"This isn't OnlyFans you know," I spat at them.

A few looked sheepish and shifted their phones and necks back to the classic shape of those consuming the interwebs. A couple got up and moved down the aisle to another car. One took a picture. I heard the click the phone company adds to make sure perverts can't do up skirts on subways, but I skewered them with my nastiest dirty look until they saw the light and went back to using their phone as a personal entertainment device rather than a broadcaster of the world to the world. Father Jim seemed oblivious to all of it. If Benito noticed, he sure didn't seem to care.

"Did you tell anyone where we were going?" I asked.

Father Jim laughed, a strained grunt.

"I live alone in a rectory. Who would I tell?"

Sweat was glistening on his brow.

"They knew I was there somehow," I said.

Father Jim didn't answer. He just kept pumping out pushups and whispering rapid fire Hail Mary's.

"I'm not your friend, dickface," declared Benito.

He was holding the iPad close to his face, his eyes wide and his tongue sticking slightly out with concentration. Father Jim rose and sat down in the seat next to Benito, wiping the sweat on his brow with the sleeve of his black button down.

"What's he watching?" I asked.

It wasn't any of the Dirty Harry films. I pretty much had those down by heart. Father Jim leaned slightly to look over Benito's shoulder.

"Looks like Bloodsport."

"Is that really the best movie to let Benito Mussolini watch?"

Father Jim shrugged. The flat landscape of the Midwest flashed by outside. Broken industrial towns divided by fields of growing corn and soybeans.

"What's with you and the old violent movies?" I asked.

"I get to be a complex person," answered Father Jim.

"What the hell is a Dim Mak?!" declared Benito.

The sharpness of the exclamation must have hurt his throat. He released a hacking cough.

We all sat in silence, Father Jim and I watching the dull scenery move by, both lost in our own worlds. Eventually a steward came down the aisle with a snack cart. I bought an overpriced bag of replacement chips and some water. My two compatriots watched me. I opened

the bag. Benito licked his lips. I held them toward Father
Jim. He politely shook his head no. I did the same with
Benito. He grabbed the entire bag and went back to his
movie.

"Time to separate the men from the boys," he
proclaimed.

I thought about saying something, but in the end
decided a quiet fascist dictator was a better fascist dictator. I
settled back into my seat. Father Jim looked at me and
raised his eyebrows in the universal sign of can you believe
this fricking guy. I couldn't help but smirk a bit. It made me
feel like a jackass.

'I'm sorry for being an asshole," I said. "You've been
doing nothing but helping me and I've just been the worst."

He shrugged.

"It's okay. We all have our moments. You should have
seen the way I yelled at my last deacon for failing to spot me
correctly. I mean, to be fair, he was eighty-two years old."

I laughed. Father Jim laughed too.

"Why are you helping me out so much?" I asked.

Father Jim leaned forward and put his square chin into
his bulky hands.

"It's the Christian thing to do. That's kind of a big part
of the whole priest thing."

He looked kind of uncomfortable.

"Plus," he added, "it feels like people like me owe people
like you a lot for all the bullshit."

I involuntarily clenched a good part of my lower body. I
had wondered if he had noticed, and if so, how much he had
noticed. I mean, I don't go out of my way to announce such
things, and I'm not the most obvious in the world, but I don't
go out of my way to hide them either. You spend days in
close quarters with someone, you're bound to notice
something.

"How did you know?" I asked tentatively.

Father Jim shrugged. His face was as red as a kid caught stealing cookies.

"I know I'm a good looking guy," he said.

So most likely he knew one, but not the other. I couldn't help but smile again.

"Not really my type," I answered.

Father Jim just shrugged again. It was like watching two mirrored mountains rise and fall. I don't think I've ever seen anyone shrug as much as him. It was as though his very existence was an inconvenience.

The world kept slipping past. Our eyes creeped away to the monotonous outer world. Father Jim pulled a small travel pack of Kleenex out of his bag and blew his nose. I crossed and uncrossed my legs, uncertain if I was crossing them too tight or not tight enough, old uncertainties returning.

"Does it bother you that I'm queer?" I asked, a bit of an edge to my voice.

Father Jim crossed his arms in front of him and leaned back into his seat. He waited several heartbeats before he pivoted his head toward me.

"Are you trying to pick up me up?"

We stared at each other. His face was empty of emotion. I struggled to decide how to answer. I wanted to answer the question in the right way. The edge of his mouth began to quiver. I laughed. He laughed too. It felt nice to laugh with him.

"No, I told you," I said, "you're not my type. When it comes to men I'm more of a chubby chaser."

Father Jim nodded his head.

"Good, because I'm celibate."

We both laughed again.

"That must make you Frank Dux," trumpeted Benito.

The train car shook a bit from side to side. I took a drink of my water. Father Jim opened his mouth, closed it, and then opened it again.

"Can I ask one thing?"

I dipped my water bottle toward him.

"Sure."

Father Jim was blushing once again.

"It might not be appropriate, but I've always been curious."

I gave him a smile.

"It would have to be pretty inappropriate for me."

Father Jim blushed clear to his ears. He really wasn't my type, but it was kind of cute how bashful he was being. Like a middle school Hercules or something.

"Okay," he said, pausing for a moment. "Why do some people say LGBTQ and others just say queer?"

I laughed.

"That's a whole can of worms," I chortled.

Father Jim leaned in. The man was a good listener.

Part 10 - Il Filantropo

It was a twenty hour train ride to New York City. Benito just watched Bloodsport again and again, though he did drink multiple pops and eat several bags of chips, all paid for by me, finally falling asleep with his entire front covered in crumbs. A couple of times my phone rang, someone with an unknown number calling, but I never answered and they never left a message. Father Jim and I talked, slept, got food from the dining car, and talked some more. By the time the train pulled into the station in the Big Apple, I was beyond glad he was with me.

I bought everyone some pre-made sandwiches at a train station kiosk and then we rode the subway into the Bronx. The name of the adoption agency was Hey, I'm Barking Here. We had to hang out in the morning frost for a while to wait for it to open.

"Who the hell are these scumbags?!" snapped Benito when he saw the slightly chunky middle-aged woman who ran the place approaching.

I recognized her from the group's website.

"She couldn't do more than one-oh-five," murmured Father Jim.

When the woman got to the door where we were waiting, she gave us the up and down, her eyes lingering on Father Jim's pecs and arms, straining through his shirt.

"Can I help you?" she asked, her voice a bit nasally.

Her eyes never left Father Jim's physique. I could see her running her tongue across her teeth under her upper lip.

"We're looking for a dog," I said.

She reluctantly turned her gaze from Father Jim to me.

"Well, you've come to the right place," she laughed, giving Father Jim a wink as she offered her hand to him.

"Lerna. Lerna with an E."

Father Jim took her hand in his big one.

"Father Jim," he said.

She smiled at him and held on until the priest broke away. She gave another laugh and unlocked the door. It was a small front office, just about enough room for a couple of chairs and a desk with a door into a backroom where, at least judging by the barking, was where the dogs were kept. Lerna made her way behind the desk and turned on her computer.

"Apologies for all the noise," she said, gesturing toward the closed door. "Carlos hasn't gotten in to feed them yet."

She gave Father Jim another smile.

"So what kind of dog are you looking for?"

"A Jack Russell," I said.

Lerna shot me a dirty look and then redirected her gaze to my well muscled companion, who was obviously feeling pretty awkward about all the attention.

"Those are quite popular," she told him. "Especially amongst the middle-aged folks who grew up with Wishbone. You know, that dog that used to tell stories."

"I have no idea what you're talking about," replied Father Jim.

"I'm more of a bigger dog fan myself," said Lerna, really drawing out the word bigger.

"I like lions!" loudly declared Benito. "Roar!"

"Is she okay?" asked Lerna.

"Aren't you a little old for video games?" replied Benito.

Lerna stared at Benito, unsure of how to take an old lady, who to the best of her judgement must have had a startlingly strange form of dementia or something. For his part, Benito raised his eyebrows and waggled them appreciatively, liking the view I guess. Lerna frowned, her face twisted by a combination of concern and confusion.

"We're looking for a specific Jack Russell," I interjected before things could go further off the rails. "He likely showed up the other day."

Lerna shook her head as though to clear it and finally gave her attention to me. Her voice was flat and a bit annoyed.

"I remember that dog. He nipped the shit out of Carlos. Bit of a bad attitude. I thought we were going to have to send him down the road, but some woman came and got him."

She turned her attention back to Father Jim.

"Probably a big Wishbone fan or something," she said with a wink.

"I remember Benji," offered Father Jim. "He made crooks think a house was haunted or something like that."

"You don't look that old," said Lerna, leaning forward on her desk and putting her chin in one of her hands.

"Le donne formose sanno come accontentare un uomo,"[49] declared Benito.

"I didn't watch a lot of TV growing up," explained Father Jim.

"Roar!" roared Benito.

---

[49] Curvy women know how to please a man.

"Can we have the address of the woman who adopted him?" I asked.

Lerna huffed and turned back toward me.

"It's against policy for us to hand out personal information."

I gestured toward Father Jim.

"It's his dog. He'd do anything to get him back."

Lerna turned back toward Father Jim, her head cranked a bit to the side, a hungry grin on her face.

"Is that so?" asked Lerna with a slow and intrigued tone.

Father Jim's eyes went wide.

"Can we talk for a moment?" he asked, gesturing with his hand for me to follow him into the far corner of the room.

I followed and Benito came too, I guess deciding that he would be needed as well. All three of us huddled in the corner.

"What are you doing?" Father Jim hissed at me.

"Getting the information we need," I whispered back. "She's obviously into you."

We looked behind ourselves at Lerna. She was pretending to type on her keyboard but was obviously giving herself a full from the corner of the eye helping of Father Jim's well-toned ass.

"I don't think we should be encouraging her," he murmured.

"Just give her a little razzle dazzle," I whispered.

"I take her like Albania," offered Benito.

"I took an oath of celibacy," mumbled Father Jim.

"No one is saying sleep with her. Do you want to find the dog or not?"

We looked behind us again. Lerna was openly staring now, doing that thing again where she ran her tongue between her upper teeth and lip.

"Culo come un prosciutto ben stagionato,"[50] hissed Benito.

Father Jim gave an audible sigh.

"Fine."

We broke the huddle. Father Jim sucked in a breath, squared his shoulders, and strode back over to the desk. Lerna eagerly watched every step.

"His name is Peaches," he said. "Is there any way we can get the address of the woman who adopted him?"

"It's against policy," repeated Lerna in a girlish voice.

"I love anything full contact," loudly whispered Benito in my ear. "I need a few more scars on my face."

Benito ran his tongue across his thin lips. I took a sidestep to the left to create a bit of space between us. Father Jim looked at me, a despairing look in his eye, took in a second resolute breath, turned back to Lerna, and then plunged into the void.

"Surely we can figure something out," he said in his most suave voice, which was pretty good overall, you know, for a celibate person.

I could practically hear Lerna ruin her chair. She gave a huge grin and seemed to shake with nervous delight.

"Okay," she said, running her hands across her small desk, "this might sound a bit weird, but is there any way we could take some pictures?"

Father Jim's eyes went wide again, but he managed to keep the charming smile plastered on.

"What kind of pictures?"

A bead of sweat trickled down his temple.

"Oh nothing dirty," she assured him, leaning forward again. "It's just, this whole super buff man of God thing is really checking a lot of boxes if you know what I mean, and I'm a bit of an amateur shutterbug."

---

[50] Ass like a well-seasoned ham.

"Oookkkaayyy," said Father Jim, really drawing out the word.

Lerna didn't need anything else. With a shy giggle she rose from her chair, grabbed him by the hand, and led him through the door into the dog kennel area, the volume of the barking rising with the opening of the door.

"Would it be too much to ask for you to chastise me like I'm an altar boy who didn't use enough incense in the thurible?" she asked as she pulled him through the door.

Father Jim gave us one last despairing look and then he was gone, the door shutting behind him, once again muffling the excited yelps of those within.

"Quel topo nero è una sgualdrina,"[51] said Benito, smiling at me.

They were gone for around half an hour or more. Benito and I waited, sitting in the chairs, me waiting impatiently with my arms crossed, him watching Bloodsport again on the iPad. At one point Benito began swinging his arms around like he was doing karate, jiggling the loose skin under his arms and yelling HI-YAH over and over, but he calmed down and went back to watching silently.

After about fifteen minutes, a short thin boned man with a little moustache came in. Given his air of belonging I can only assume he was Carlos. He gave us a quizzical look, so I pointed at the door leading to the dog kennels, which seemed to be enough for him because he walked over and went in without a word. For a moment, through the briefly open door, I saw Father Jim standing with his shirt off, Lerna's rounded form in his arms, head thrown back as though she was somehow stricken and he was lifting her to safety. The man who I assumed to be Carlos did not even hesitate to walk inside.

---

[51] That black mouse is a slut.

"One-fifteen," I thought I heard Father Jim say as the assumed Carlos walked in.

Then the door closed and I saw nothing more.

When Father Jim finally came back into the office he looked distraught and smelled of wet dog food. Lerna's hair was out of sorts and she was quite flushed and grinning like an idiot.

"You cannot take katana sword by stealing," laughed Benito. "It is very special sword, you must earn it."

Lerna tapped at her computer a bit, wrote down the address on a piece of paper, and handed it to the priest, her hand lingering against his in its passing.

"You come back any time."

Father Jim gave a smile full of gritted teeth, nodded, and then turned and started for the exit. I rose, dragging Benito by his bony elbow.

"If you give me your email, I'll send you copies of…" called out Lerna, but the closing door cut her off.

Part 11 – Grande Mela

We all walked in silence for a few blocks until I finally got up the nerve to speak.

"What happened in there?"

His eyes were far away.

"So many judgey dogs."

He said nothing more. He just led us to the nearest subway station and down into the depths.

Father Jim began doing sit ups and reciting Our Fathers as soon as the subway train started moving. People gave him a wide berth. I couldn't really blame them. I can't imagine it's everyday you see an overly muscled priest willingly laying on the floor of a New York City subway car.

For my part I sat next to Benito. He was still completely enamored with Bloodsport, but I wasn't much interested in watching a twenty-seven year old action flick, especially one without sound, so I mostly took in some people watching. New York City definitely did not have a shortage of people worth watching. There were two women in matching zebra tights and neon aquamarine wigs. There was a guy in a full tuxedo even though it was mid-morning. There was a woman holding a leash attached to a collar around a guy's neck, though that was something I have seen many times if I'm being honest. There was a priest doing sit ups, though you already knew that. There was a woman wearing the same outfit as the pug dog in her arms, and there was one guy dressed up like an unshaven white version of Prince, may he rest in peace, 1999 definitely being on my all time greatest playlist. The Prince guy evidently did not enjoy my eyes resting for too long on his amazing get up.

"What are ya lookin at?" he yelled with a thick Brooklyn accent.

I quickly glanced away, but he was already approaching, squeezing his way past people who, aside from a few side eyes, completely ignored the interaction.

"Youse think you can just ogle people ya fuckin bastard!" he yelled in my face.

Prince swung a fist toward my head. He stopped an inch from my nose. I didn't flinch. Years of being bullied in school had ingrained in me the need to never flinch. To just take it. Someone rose up next to me. For a split second I was sure it was Father Jim, but it wasn't. It was Benito, his eyes flashing with red hot anger.

"Che cazzo credi di essere?!" he screamed right into Prince's face. "Va' a farti fottere!"[52]

Prince's face turned a bright furious red.

"Youse don't think I understand Italian, you pezzo di merda!"[53] he yelled. "Tu, vecchia puttana dalle tette flosce!"[54]

"Tuo padre era un cornuto e lo sanno tutti!" screamed Benito. "Fanculo tua madre, come fanno tutti gli altri!"[55]

---

[52] What the fuck do you think you are? Go fuck yourself!
[53] Piece of shit!
[54] You old floppy-titted whore!
[55] Your father was a cuckold and everyone knows it! Fuck your mother, like everyone else does!

Prince pushed Benito back down onto the bench. Benito rose up and pushed Prince back.

"Enough!" yelled Father Jim.

His mouth was set in a stern line. His voice was a commanding roar. He stepped between the two combatants.

"You," he ordered, putting a hand on Benito and pushing him back down, "sit down."

Then he turned upon Prince.

"And you," he commanded, bringing his full bulk in close to the other man, "go to the other side of the car and leave us alone."

For a moment it looked as though Prince was going to give Father Jim a go, but then he just grunted, turned his back, and walked away. Father Jim watched him. Everyone else in the car found something else to look at.

"Avrei potuto batterlo," muttered Benito. "Non ho bisogno di un topo nero che mi protegga."[56]

"Quiet," ordered Father Jim, pointing a beefy finger at the frail woman next to me.

Benito huffed, and then just chuckled to himself. Father Jim went back to doing sit ups and Our Fathers. Benito looked over and kindly patted me on the knee.

"You didn't flinch!" he said. "You have fighting spirit!"

I felt strangely pleased at the compliment, even if he was just quoting what was in my opinion a terrible movie.

"Thank you."

"Se fossi stato ancora al comando dell'Italia, avremmo alimentato forzatamente quel ragazzo con olio di ricino finché non avesse cagato e fosse morto."[57]

"I see," I answered, figuring it was politer to pretend I understood.

---

[56] I could have beaten him. I don't need a black mouse to protect me.

[57] If I were still in charge of Italy, we would have force-fed that boy castor oil until he shit and died.

"Come minimo avremmo sparato a lui e poi alla sua famiglia, per sicurezza,"[58] he added.

I just kind of smiled and nodded.

"Avevo dei testicoli enormi,"[59] sighed Benito.

I just shrugged and gave her knee a gentle shake.

---

[58] At the very least we would have shot him and then his family, just to be safe.

[59] I had huge testicles.

Part 12 - Letto Condiviso

It was a confusing series of subway trains that zigzagged us from the Bronx deep into Brooklyn. We had some difficulty finding the apartment we were looking for, what with us not thinking to look under a stairwell, but eventually we found it. When we knocked, a very stoned looking older gentleman sporting a greasy gray beard and a Nuke the Whales t-shirt opened the door, his eyes growing wide at the sight of Father Jim.

"Ninety-five," murmured Father Jim.

"Whhoooaaa," said the older gentleman. "Tell Matlock I'm all paid up man, no need to send out the goon squad."

He went to shut the door, but I stuck my foot in the way.

"We're here to see Kylie," I tried to explain.

The older gentleman pulled back open the door.

"Cool, cool," he muttered, staring vacantly at us.

"Is she here?" I asked, trying to keep my patience.

"Yep."

"Can we see her?"

I was starting to get a bit perturbed.

"You'd better stop doing that," said Benito, his fist waving in the air. "You might wanna have kids one of these days."

"What's up with your crazy grandma, buddy?" asked the older gentleman.

"Kylie?" I asked again.

"Yeah man, she lives here."

I took in a sharp breath. I swear I was going to punch the guy right in the mouth.

"Can we speak to her?" asked Father Jim, calmly interjecting himself into the conversation.

"Of course Father," replied the older gentleman with a smile. "I'll go get her."

He left the door open and went back inside. Father Jim just shrugged at me. Inside the apartment wasn't much to look at. We could basically see the whole thing from the open doorway. A single room with an unfolded fold out couch, a small kitchenette with the slimmest fridge I'd ever seen and a two burner stove, and a flowered shower curtain hiding what appeared to be a shower in one corner. It was to this corner that the older stoned gentleman strolled, pulling open the curtain to reveal a young woman sitting on a toilet built into the shower, her pants still up, reading a book.

"Someone at the door for you," he said.

Message delivered, he ambled over and laid down on the pull out. Fun fact, the best bar trivia team name I ever heard was My Couch Pulls Out But I Don't, but that's not important right now.

The young woman put a marker in her book that appeared to be made out of a braided piece of her own hair, put the book down on the floor, rose, and walked toward us. She was wearing a large crystal on a cord around her neck. She was also not wearing a bra, though of course that's not an appropriate way to describe a woman, you know, but it was pretty damn noticeable.

"Yum, yum," said Benito.

"Also ninety-five," murmured Father Jim.

"Are you Kylie?" I asked.

"Yes."

She brushed a long piece of hair behind her ear. She had unusually large and pale blue eyes and a very intense stare. When she spoke, it was with a tone I would describe as bemused boredom.

"What's with Benito Mussolini?" she asked.

Father Jim and I looked at each other, both of us startled.

"She's just an old woman," I stated.

"How did you know?" asked Father Jim simultaneously.

I shot Father Jim a dirty look. He gave me one of those my bad faces where you show your teeth and widen your eyes.

"Finalmente il rispetto che merito!"[60] laughed Benito, his face split by a wide smile revealing his overly stereotypical English teeth.

The young woman simply stared at us with her giant eyes.

"The musician?" called out the older gentleman from the pull out.

"That's Romano Mussolini," she replied.

She rolled her eyes and absentmindedly twisted the crystal around her neck on its cord.

"This one's his dad, the fascist dictator," she added nonchalantly. "The architect of the Libyan genocide. The releaser of chemical weapons in Abyssinia. The bulldog who re-introduced child labor. The man who killed off political opponents, dissidents, communists, gypsies, and Jews to the tune of thousands."

---

[60] Finally the respect I deserve!

"Oh," said the older gentleman, not really seeming all that interested anymore.

"Jesus Christ," said Father Jim.

"Yeah," said the young woman, "he probably killed around half a million people, probably twice that if you count all his own soldiers and people who died in needless wars."

She stared at us like we were idiots or something. I swear Benito was crying in what, at least judging by his beaming smile, were tears of joy, which made my skin crawl to no end and filled me with an overwhelming urge to wash the hand which had shaken his knee earlier.

"I mean," she continued, "how would one not recognize such a monster?"

Father Jim's eyes were wide and his boyish face was pale.

"I knew he was bad," he stammered. "You know, torture and trampling on human rights and the such, but you just don't hear really that much about him."

He rubbed his temples with a single beefy hand and shook his head as if to clear it.

"How do you know all this?" he asked with sudden intense curiosity.

The young woman lifted one eyebrow a bit, a small smile slit her lips.

"Serial killers, mass shooters, and brutal dictators are kind of my guilty pleasure."

"Il mio tipo di donna,"[61] said Benito.

Father Jim started saying a prayer under his breath.

"Especially second rate ones," she added.

"Opinions are like assholes," spit Benito. "Everybody has one."

---

[61] My type of woman.

He seemed especially proud of himself for that one. I don't think it was from a movie. I'm not sure where he heard it from. I felt the need to puke.

"So why is he in an old lady's body?" asked the young woman. "Does this have something to do with the old lady in the dog?"

Father Jim stopped praying. My need to puke lessened.

"Is the dog here?" I demanded, my voice cracking a bit in excitement.

"It's with Kylie," answered the young woman.

"I thought you were Kylie," pointed out Father Jim.

"I'm Kylie J. You're looking for Kylie M."

"I'm also a Kylee," offered the older gentleman from the couch, "just with an E instead of an I."

"She's at work," said Kylie J., ignoring Kylee.

"She took the dog to work?" I asked.

"She tells everyone it's a service dog," said the older gentleman from the couch, whose Nuke the Whales shirt had ridden up revealing a steel gray treasure trail. "Not cool man. Not cool."

Kylie J. rolled her eyes again.

"Can you tell us where she works?" I asked.

She sauntered slowly back to her book, ripped out a blank back page, then made her way to the kitchenette and opened a drawer to find a pen.

"Three people in here," whispered Father Jim. "Do you think they all sleep on the pull out or something?"

"Just a big cuddle puddle man," called out the older gentleman, picking lint from his belly button.

"Quel drogato deve saperci fare con la vagina,"[62] declared Benito.

"Shut up," I ordered.

---

[62] That junkie must know his way around a vagina.

"Just be sure Benito doesn't separate your head from your body," Benito growled back.

"Shut up you bitch," ordered Father Jim, putting pressure on Benito's elderly shoulder with his big hand.

Kylie J. strolled back to us and handed over the ripped out page.

"Has he said anything about syphilis?" asked Kylie J., not looking disinterested for the first time since we'd seen her. "I've read he went all crazy because of untreated syphilis."

"Il mio cazzo è pulito come quello di una vergine..."[63] proclaimed Benito.

"I said shut up," ordered Father Jim, giving Benito's shoulder another squeeze.

"I have no idea," I answered. "He mostly just speaks Italian."

"And quotes from Bloodsport and all five Dirty Harry films," muttered the priest.

Kylie J. looked disappointed. She slowly closed the door in our faces.

"Let's go," said Father Jim.

---

[63] My cock is clean like a virgin's...

Part 13 – Sifilide

The subway ride into Manhattan was a quiet
one. When we first got on, Benito reached over to take the
iPad and headphones from Father Jim's bag, but he refused
to hand them over. Benito started struggling, making
whining sounds like a sleeping dog having nightmares, but
Father Jim just pushed him back with one of his strong
hands. Benito began to shake with frustration. He rose from
his seat and stomped his foot like a child.

"Dammi i miei film, stupido topo nero!"[64] he yelled.

Father Jim did his best to ignore him.

"Se non mi restituisci i miei film ti ammazzo come tutti
quei libici!"[65] he screamed, stomping his foot again.

Benito was turning very red in the face. I was
beginning to wonder if maybe he was going to have a heart
attack or something. Agatha Christie's body didn't seem all
that healthy from the looks of it.

---

[64] Give me my movies, you stupid black mouse!
[65] If you don't give me back my films I'll kill you like all those
Libyans!

"Maybe we should..." I started to say, but stopped mid sentence, a single glare from Father Jim making me swallow the words.

"Sit down," he ordered Benito.

The old lady body jumped up and down, spittle flying from his mouth.

"Lo voglio!," Benito screamed. "Lo voglio! Lo voglio adesso!"[66]

He scrambled for the iPad, but Father Jim pushed him away, not as gently as before.

"Enough!" he yelled.

He took out the iPad and for a moment Benito calmed, believing he was about to get his way, but then Father Jim gripped it with both hands and broke it in half as easily as a child snapping a cracker. Benito screamed a long terrible scream and prepared himself to rush forward.

"Go ahead," Father Jim growled, "make my day!"

"Dim mak!" yelled Benito.

He charged forward, throwing all of his weight into it. He might as well have been throwing an old lumpy pillow at the muscle bound priest. Father Jim pushed him down into the seat with the same effort he used to raise a glass of water to his lips. People were watching us, waiting to see what would happen. A few had their phones out, one or two obviously recording.

"Sit down and stay down," Father Jim whispered, leaning in close.

Benito began to cry. Long hard sobs that shook his entire body.

"Voglio morire!" he screamed. "Preferirei tornare all'inferno piuttosto che avere a che fare con questa merda!"[67]

---

[66] I want it! I want it! I want it now!

[67] "I want to die! I'd rather go back to hell than deal with this shit!

Father Jim looked up and saw the phones. He rose and looked down at his feet, breathing, getting himself back under control. He cut his hand through the air above Benito's head, making the sign of the cross.

"Out demon, get out!" he said in a loud voice.

A couple of people laughed. Father Jim kept his head bent down over the sobbing Benito. I could see his lips moving as though he was praying silently, but from my vantage point it looked more like he was cursing over and over. People waited to see what else would happen. I rose.

"That's our show," I declared. "If you're interested in seeing more we'll be performing The Priest and the Prima Donna, an original stage play, at the Blalock Repertory Theater all this week!"

People averted their eyes as though I were a beggar on the street. They lowered their phones, bent their necks, and went back into themselves. The subway stopped and people got on and people got off. Father Jim went down the aisle a bit and put himself into a plank position. I could hear him reciting the Apostles' Creed, the words coming out in short bursts. Benito was still crying, but no longer sobbing, his head tucked against the window, his watery eyes fixated on the blackness of the tunnel outside, or perhaps his wrinkled reflection. I got up and made my way down the aisle, sitting down in the seat closest to Father Jim's head.

"That wasn't very Christian of you," I observed.

Father Jim didn't bother to raise his head.

"Given how you got him, I'd say he's already been judged, wouldn't you?"

I looked back down the train to make sure Benito hadn't moved.

"Where's the Blalock Theater?" Father Jim asked.

The corner of my mouth twitched.

"That was my high school theater teacher's name. God, how he was a pain in the ass. The man was obsessed with The Pirates of Penzance."

Father Jim didn't answer. He was still staring at the floor.

"Should we be worried about all that?" I asked.

"Your theater teacher is probably dead by now," replied Father Jim.

"Some of those people had cameras," I pointed out.

Father Jim just chuckled.

"The Church is very forgiving, perhaps at times too forgiving."

I could see little drops of sweat forming on his brow. I said nothing for a while, but I didn't want to go sit next to Benito and watching a man do a plank for minutes on end feels awkward, so I began to try and think of something else to say. Luckily Father Jim beat me to the punch.

"I shouldn't have acted the way I did." His voice sounded a bit strained. "I think I was more mad at myself for being so willfully ignorant."

I smiled, but of course he couldn't see it.

"Well," I answered, "I mean he was a terrible monster who killed thousands of people."

Father Jim let himself drop to the floor and then rolled himself into a sitting position.

"The Bible teaches us the importance of forgiveness, but I don't think I can forgive somebody like him."

I bit my bottom lip.

"Maybe it's okay not to forgive," I suggested. "Maybe not everyone needs to be forgiven. I mean, would he have been in Hell if he was worthy of forgiveness?"

Father Jim wiped the sweat off his face with the upper parts of his black sleeves, dipping his head toward his shoulders, one side and then the other.

"Or maybe it's not our place to forgive him," I continued. "I mean, yeah, he's been most definitely a monster, and we should totally judge him for that, but we aren't his victims. We aren't the ones who were hurt. Thinking about this from our perspective in terms of forgiveness just seems wrong."

Father Jim dried his hands on his pants legs.

"Maybe," he said, "but it seems that if we judge, and we treat someone differently based upon those judgements, then we have put ourselves in a position where that person must earn our forgiveness as well as those they actually hurt."

"Are there levels of hurt where there can be no forgiveness no matter what?" I asked. "I mean, isn't that the purpose of Hell?"

"Maybe, but then that would mean there is no chance for redemption at a certain point. And if that's true, then when one hits that certain point there is no reason not to turn back. There is no reason not to double down."

I leaned back and tapped my head against the scratched glass of the window.

"I mean, could the Devil himself be redeemed?" I asked.

Father Jim was staring at the darkness outside the window behind me.

"I don't know," he said. "They don't cover things like this in Seminary school as well as you'd think."

I chuckled.

"So much for spiritual infallibility."

"You don't know the half of it," he answered with a half-smile.

We sat in silence for a bit again, both of us glancing from time to time up the car to make sure Benito was still where we had left him. We couldn't tell if he was sleeping or still pouting.

"Do you think what Kylie J. said is true?" I asked.

Father Jim looked at me, his head slightly tilted to the side.

"How do you mean?"

"About the whole syphilis thing." I tapped my skull with a finger. "That part of why he was such a monster being that syphilis had rotted his brain."

Father Jim shrugged. It was nice to see him shrugging. It was such an affable motion, a declaration that he did not know everything and was okay with having others know it.

"Possibly. I've heard both Al Capone and Howard Hughes had it, and they were both nuttier than fruitcakes."

I leaned forward and rubbed my forehead a bit. My head was starting to hurt a bit.

"Does that mean that maybe he's not the same person now that he's in a different body?"

"Benito is Benito," answered Father Jim without hesitation. "What we call Benito is his soul, not the corporeal form he inhabits."

"Yeah, but syphilis is not an ailment of the soul," I replied. "It's a sickness of the body. Which means if he was in a different body wouldn't it be possible that he would have acted differently?"

Father Jim was staring out at the darkness again. There were creases on his forehead.

"I think we are all culpable for what we do, regardless of the circumstances. Bad circumstances are not a carte blanche excuse for bad behavior."

"But if he was truly mentally ill," I pressed, "if it was a defect or side effect that if he was born in a different time and place, could have been avoided or fixed, would that make a difference?"

The priest looked up the car at Benito. He gave out a half grunt and half sigh and rose up from the floor without using his hands. He looked down at me and shrugged.

"I don't think it's going to matter much longer either way."

He started to move up the aisle but then turned back.

"I also don't think that not a racist factoid I said earlier this week was probably accurate either."

He turned and moved up the aisle back towards Benito, slightly unsteadied by the rock of the subway car. When he reached the pieces of broken iPad he crouched down, picked them up, and put them into his bag.

Benito

Part 14 - Sosta Caffè

The coffee shop where we sat was one of those industrial chic kinds of places, with minimalist furnishings nestled amongst excessively large potted plants, all under a ceiling of exposed wires and duct work. It was a big place, much bigger than you would think it would need to be. The price for a cup of coffee was so ridiculous I won't even get into it, because you know how long I can go on when it comes to the price of a cup of coffee. I like my coffee like I like my lovers. Simple, old fashioned, and cheap as hell. And I mean simple as in the opposite of fancy, not stupid. Nobody wants to hang out with stupid people, no matter how good looking they are, except for my friend Emily. She calls them hush babies, as in hush baby, talking is not what you're here for. To each their own I guess. This is a pretty long way of saying that I was drinking my drip coffee black. Father Jim was drinking some tea and eating a piece of cake.

"Do you want to have some?" he had asked.

"No thank you," I had answered.

"It's sssoooo good," he said, drawing out the middle like an excited middle schooler.

Benito, though still sulking over his movies being taken away, was drinking a frappuccino covered by an impressive mound of whipped cream, something he had managed to order entirely via gesturing and grunting like a toddler. When he got it, Father Jim had expressed the opinion that mass murderers probably shouldn't get to enjoy their preferred coffee beverages.

"You are next," had declared Benito, giving the priest the evil eye. "Ballerai per me quando ti impiccheranno."[68]

I made the executive decision to give him what he wanted, because it was my money being spent and because I figured our lives would be easier if we just gave him the fricking frappuccino.

We had been sitting in the coffee shop for over an hour. Across the street was a high rise jamming itself impudently into the sky, one of many. Box trucks were parked in front, with men wearing back braces and taking a copious number of breaks. Unloading lights, cables, cameras, and other such audio visual equipment and taking them inside the building when they weren't standing around. Security guards milled about. Mostly cheap ones in ballistic vests and baseball caps, but also some higher value individuals in suits and sunglasses. It had been Father Jim who had noticed the latter.

"What other kind of person just stands around in a suit?" he asked.

This was where Kylie M. worked.

"How the hell are we going to get into that place?" I asked.

Father Jim shrugged, taking a sip from his tea, the movements in unison.

"I don't know. Quite a few of those guys could probably bench over two hundred."

---

[68] You'll dance for me when they hang you.

I looked over at Benito who was happily sucking on the straw jammed into his drink. He noticed me looking and gave me a dirty look.

"You getting an eyeful, you goddamn pie hocker."

Benito was part way through his third frappuccino when Father Jim slapped his big hand down onto the table.

"I've got it. I knew if I did a bit of exercising I'd figure it out."

"What exercising?" I asked. "You've just been sitting there drinking tea."

"Kegels," he said with a big wide grin.

"Kegels," I repeated stupidly.

"Nobody likes an old incontinent priest," replied Father Jim with a wink.

"Sono abbastanza sicuro che questa vecchia signora abbia qualcosa che non va nel duodeno."[69]

"Shut up," ordered Father Jim.

"Il mio vecchio corpo aveva un duodeno malato," muttered Mussolini. "Dovevo sempre fare la cacca."[70]

Father Jim gave him a hard look. Benito grumbled to himself and gave his straw a long loud suck.

"So what's the plan?" I asked.

Father Jim told me the plan. When he finished, I looked at him, wondering if maybe I should tell him to go back to doing kegels until he came up with something better.

"It will work," he promised.

"We could always wait for her to come out," I suggested.

"Figa,"[71] said Benito, sneering at me.

I didn't understand the word, but I recognized its delivery.

---

[69] I'm pretty sure this old lady has something wrong with her duodenum.

[70] My old body had a diseased duodenum. I had to poop all the time.

[71] Pussy.

"Look here…" I said leaning forward, my finger pointed at his face.

"I think we're going to have to try it," interrupted Father Jim, pointing at the door to the street.

The door was just opening with a happy jangle. Two men in old pea coats and pork pie hats walked in.

"Sociology?" murmured Benito with a feral grin. "Oh, you'll go far. That's if you live."

Part 15 - Torre Dorata

Nigel and The Grip didn't see us, as we were too nestled in amongst the greenery. However, their piggy eyes traced their way across everything as they moved deeper into the coffee shop. Nigel looked tired, his clothes rumpled and his hat a bit smashed on one side. The Grip looked less travel worn, but when he flashed a feral grin to frighten a seated couple staring at him and his partner, there was a black gap in his golden grill.

"How the frick did they find us?" I hissed.

Father Jim didn't answer. He was too busy stretching his arms and shoulders, getting himself ready.

"Divertitevi a restare appesi per le caviglie in una stazione di servizio,"[72] said Benito in a menacing voice, giving us a sinister grin.

I didn't like how that sounded. I thought about flipping him off or maybe even giving him a good bop in the nose, but then I saw what we needed behind him.

"The door," I hissed.

---

[72] Have fun hanging by your ankles at a gas station.

Nigel was up at the counter, talking to the young zit covered kid behind it. The Grip was moving a glittering eye across the coffee shop interior. He was obviously enjoying his work.

"They're too close to the door," whispered back Father Jim.

"Stazione di servizio, stazione di servizio, stazione di servizio,"[73] wheezed Benito, his eyes wide, a sheen of sweat setting his face aglow.

"Not that door," I hissed. "That one."

I grabbed Father Jim's big shoulder and pulled him around, my finger pointing at the single glass door tucked away behind us by the bathrooms. His eyes widened with understanding. Nigel raised his voice. It was much raspier than it had been before. Our heads whipped back around in unison. Nigel was getting into some kind of argument with the zit covered kid. Everyone in the place turned their heads to watch. The Grip began making his way to his partner's side.

"Let's go," I insisted in a strained whisper.

"È come di nuovo l'Egitto,"[74] muttered Benito.

We rose into a crouch, both Father Jim and I grabbing hold of either side of Benito to propel him along. The moment we were up a middle-aged woman with a latte and an expensive looking haircut approached.

"Are you done with this table?" she asked pleasantly in a surprisingly loud voice.

A couple of people turned from Nigel's commotion to look at our own.

"Eighty," murmured Father Jim.

"Shhhhhh," I hissed, raising an elevated finger to my mouth.

---

[73] Gas station, gas station, gas station.
[74] It's like Egypt all over again.

"Don't shush me," declared the middle-aged woman, raising her voice further.

"You know, you're crazy if you think you've heard the last of this guy," declared Benito, not nearly as quiet as we needed him to be. "He's gonna kill again."

The woman's mouth fell open. Father Jim hustled us toward the door.

"Sorry," he called back as we went. "Dementia. Please enjoy the table."

"Your bag!" called out the woman behind us.

She was holding up Father Jim's bag, but we were already pretty much out the door and there was no turning back. The glass door opened into the main lobby of the high rise we were in. The moment we had a wall between us and the coffee shop, we straightened up and hurried toward the big glass revolving doors leading out to the street.

"This isn't going to work," I insisted.

"Go for the stomach, and stay away from his right leg," suggested Benito.

"It's going to work," asserted Father Jim.

Any further argument was pointless. We were already making our way across the street, maneuvering Frogger like through the cars waiting for the light to turn green. I glanced back at the coffee shop from whence we came. Nigel must have really been throwing a fit. Through the big glass windows I could see a crowd thickening around the counter. A car honked. The light at the end of the block had turned green. The driver flipped us off. I looked up at the gleaming tower of glass haughtily ramming itself into the sky. Then we were in amongst the parked box trucks, and then amidst the union laborers and security guards, making our way toward the revolving golden doors.

"Hey!" ordered a nasally voice. "Hold it right there!"

All three of us flinched.

"Where do you think you're going?" interrogated the voice.

We turned.

"One-sixty," murmured Father Jim.

The nasally voice belonged to a nasally young man who couldn't have been more than his early twenties, but he had a gun at his hip and a flak jacket with Security emblazoned across his chest. One could tell just by looking at him that he was one of those security guards who really got off on the power of his position. Somebody who thought highly enough of themselves that they would do their job with a seriousness bordering on obsession. The kind of person who probably jerked off to himself in the mirror while wearing his full get-up. In other words, the worst possible person for Father Jim's plan to work.

"Un greco potrebbe battere questo cucciolo,"[75] muttered Benito.

Father Jim flashed his most innocent smile, which was impressively somehow more innocent than expected given his boyish face.

"Excuse me?"

"I said where do you think you're going?" repeated the security guard.

Father Jim turned his head slightly to the side in a quizzical manner.

"Inside," he answered in a matter of fact tone, pointing with a beefy finger.

The security guard put a hand on the butt of his gun. I did my best to appear more bored than nervous, but undoubtedly failed miserably. I'm a pretty good actor, but I usually don't have to perform under such conditions.

"What business do you have here?" questioned the security guard, his voice what I imagine he felt was

---

[75] A Greek could beat this puppy.

menacing, his back and knees slightly bending, his fingers lightly caressing his firearm.

"Ho proprio bisogno di fare pipì,"[76] declared Benito.

"Oh," said Father Jim, broadening his smile even more. "Apologies, I am Father Figaro Ferrari and I'm here to bless the set."

The security guard straightened his knees a bit.

"What?" he said, sounding a bit stupid.

"I'm here to bless the set."

"La mia vescica sta per scoppiare,"[77] stated Benito, shaking my arm.

"Bless the set?"

The security guard looked even more confused.

"You know how superstitious these film people are," said Father Jim.

The security guard's face went hard again, or at least what he must have imagined was a hard face while practicing in front of the mirror.

"This is a TV production," he said, "not a film set."

"They're even worse," declared the priest with a wink. "A few weeks ago I had to bless every camera, cable, and light. It was crazy."

The security guard smiled a bit, not meaning to, but smiling still the same.

"Tell me about it. One time a woman came here so a bunch of bigwigs could eat sushi off of her. Can you believe it? Fucking sushi!"

Father Jim gave out a jovial guffaw, which I felt was a little too much, but it seemed to relax the security guard further, so I guess it was just right.

"Who are they?" the security guard asked, gesturing toward Benito and me, still a step or two back.

---

[76] I really need to pee.
[77] My bladder is about to burst.

"That's my brother and my mother," explained the priest. "They've come to watch me work."

"Watch you work?" repeated the security guard, a hint of suspicion creeping back into his voice.

"You know how mothers are," offered Father Jim, the confidence in his voice eroding with every word.

"I'm an orphan. I'd better call this in."

He reached for the radio on his belt. Benito jerked my arm.

"Vado a farmi la pipì addosso,"[78] he whined.

He was pressing his legs together and started doing a little pee dance.

"Fiero," I interjected, "Mama needs to use the bathroom and you know what terrible UTIs she gets if she holds it too long."

The security guard paused.

"I'm trying," answered Father Jim.

"Trying doesn't keep her from screaming all night in pain when the UTIs take hold," I insisted.

The priest gave the security guard an imploring look. The beady eyes of the security guard fell on the old woman whimpering and dancing before him and then back to Father Jim.

"Maledette queste pipe da vecchia signora,"[79] cried Benito.

The security guard chewed on the insides of his cheeks. He gave Father Jim the old up and down.

"You don't look very Italian," he muttered.

"I'm Latvian on my mother's side."

"The UTIs," I insisted.

"Vorrei potervi dare tutti in pasto al mio leone,"[80] squealed Benito.

----

[78] I'm going to pee on myself.
[79] Damn these old lady pipes.
[80] I wish I could feed you all to my lion.

The security blew air out through his lips.

"Go on in," he decided, waving us forward.

"Bless you," said Father Jim.

We headed inside, Benito waddling frantically before us, the only thing keeping him from running being the bad joints of his body and the fact he would likely piss all over the floor if he went any faster.

"Told you it would work," said Father Jim with a grin.

It was in a surprisingly condescending tone for a priest, but I chose to ignore it. Benito waddled into the restroom, choosing the open portal to the men's side without hesitation, rounding the corner and disappearing. Father Jim and I loitered outside like a couple of bathroom perverts.

"Fancy place," said Father Jim, gazing around.

We were in a tall multi-floor golden lobby with matching escalators and elevators. Everything was fricking gold. The floors, the walls, everything. Union TV laborers moved about, carrying this and that, setting up for a shoot in the lobby and also disappearing and reappearing into and out of the further depths of the building.

"How are we going to find or even recognize this Kylie M.?" I asked.

Father Jim shrugged his broad shoulders.

"God will provide a sign," he said, his fricking face full of pompous grace.

I gave him a look, but he didn't notice, he was already scanning the lobby.

"Upbeat son of a bitch," I muttered.

"Eighty," he murmured.

"What?"

"There she is," he said.

He was pointing his finger at an escalator two floors up. She had bleached white hair and an outfit I could best describe as business slut. In her arms was Agatha Christie, wearing a service dog vest that looked like it had been bought online at a discount price. I couldn't fricking believe it.

"I'll go get Peaches," declared Father Jim, "you wait here for Benito."

I tried to argue, but he was already gone, rushing toward the nearest escalator, winding his way through the people with an amazingly light step for being such a bulky boy. I watched as Kylie M. and Peaches got off the escalator and moved out of sight. I watched as Father Jim got caught up behind a group of people in business attire shooting the shit and just standing on the second escalator. I watched him stand there for a moment, lose his patience, then push his way through. It was strangely delicious to watch Father Jim lose his temper. To know he was just like the rest of us.

"Stay quiet and keep ya hands where we can see em," growled a raspy voice.

Nigel and The Grip were right in front of me. They had pistols in their hands, tucked in close to their bodies so nobody else would notice. The Grip snickered. Nigel subtly gestured with his pistol for me to move toward a nearby corner with an empty set of golden chairs around a golden coffee table. I did as I was told. The Grip smiled, showing off the gap in his golden grill.

"Now then love," said Nigel, his voice low and threatening. "Where's Annis?"

Part 16 – Gli Scagnozzi

The Grip snickered again. I could feel a bead of sweat rolling down my forehead, but didn't dare move my hands to wipe it away. Nigel looked tired. He was a bit slack jawed and his eyes were puffy.

"I'll say it again," growled Nigel. "Where in Queen Vickie's nighties es Annis and where in Albert's extra tadger hole es that priest that cheap shotted me?"

I nervously let my eyes rove around, hoping I might see Father Jim. Nigel turned his head to see what I was looking at. It was a jerking nervous motion. The Grip never took his eyes off me.

"How did you find us?" I asked.

Nigel chuckled.

"My colleague here es good with computers and the such."

I wasn't sure exactly what that meant, but the Grip gave me a lurid wink and made kissy sounds with his mouth, which though not providing any further clarity, did make me decide it was better to try a different line of questioning.

"But how did you get past the security guards?" I asked, hoping to keep him talking.

Nigel rolled his eyes.

"Ow do ya think ya muppet? We gave the bloke fifty bucks. People do all sorts of things for a Ulysses S. Grant. He won yer Civil War ya know."

"Didn't Lincoln win the war?"

Nigel shook his head like I was stupid.

"Sure," he replied, "that's why they put him on the penny. Winners always end up on the smallest bits of cash."

"He's on the five too."

The Grip snickered. Nigel grunted, clearly becoming exasperated with the whole line of conversation.

"Enough," he gruffly ordered. "Where en Georgie Three's straitjacket es Annis?"

I made a big show of looking like I was thinking about it, clenching my teeth and gazing toward the ceiling.

"Enough of that tosh ma little bird," insisted Nigel.

"I have no idea," I answered.

"Saint Francis' nutty poops," he growled. "The Grip saw her on the train with ya."

Every bit of me felt soaked with sweat. The Grip seemed to be able to smell the fear on me. He took a menacing step closer.

"You're not going to believe me if I told you," I answered.

"Try me," said Nigel, "I'm an open minded..."

Nigel's watch beeped.

"Lionheart's loins!" cursed Nigel. He turned toward The Grip. "Ya need to use the loo?"

The Grip kind of shrugged then nodded.

"All right," sighed Nigel, gesturing with his head. "You go then I'll go."

The Grip put away his gun into an interior pocket on his coat and strode away toward the bathroom. I watched him go, my whole body shaking like a leaf. Nigel could see the confused look on my face. He rolled his eyes.

"Accordin to the American Brotherhood of Goons, Tough Guys, and Caricature Artists we get at least four bathroom breaks a day. I don't really care much about such things, but The Grip certainly does."

We just stood, staring at each other.

"So are we....?" I began.

"Not until he gets back," ordered Nigel.

We both turned our heads toward the bathroom, looked back at each other, and then at the bathroom again. Nigel tapped his foot impatiently.

"So ya like football?" he asked. "The world kind, not the American kind?"

Benito came out of the bathroom. She and The Grip must have just missed each other.

"Annis?" said Nigel, his voice confused, his mouth hanging open.

"Ho distrutto quel bagno come ho distrutto l'esercito albanese!"[81] yelled Benito, sticking his spindly arms into the air.

"Annis?" Nigel said again, befuddled beyond reason.

The business end of his gun wandered away. I didn't hesitate. Some people might call what I did dirty pool, but those people probably don't have guns pointed at them. I did what I did and I challenge anybody to have handled things differently. It got the job done. I kicked Nigel right in the nuts. I kicked him hard, and then when he went down, I kicked him a couple more times in the general vicinity, though it was a more difficult target given how curled up he had become. Then, for good measure I stomped on his porkpie hat where it had rolled off of his head.

"Bertie's brittle bangers!" groaned Nigel.

---

[81] I destroyed that bathroom like I destroyed the Albanian army!

I ran toward the bathroom.

"Chung Li's weak in the gut!" yelled Benito.

The Grip came out of the bathroom behind him. He didn't see me or Nigel. All of his attention was on Agatha Christie's back, which judging from his excitement, he must have known was hers. He rushed toward her. Then he saw me. He seemed a bit overwhelmed. Then Benito spun around and kicked him in the nuts.

"He's soft there!" yelled Benito.

I rushed over to them. I gave The Grip a few cursory kicks and then I was running again, dragging Benito along with me. An elevator was open. I turned to look over my shoulder as we ran. Both Nigel and The Grip were tenderly rising to their knees. I turned back toward our goal, pretty much dragging Benito as I went, expecting at any moment to hear the sounds of gunfire, but none came. We pushed our way onto the elevator just as the golden door slid shut. A tall woman who looked like a model was already on it, holding the hand of small blonde boy.

"I do not like to miss elevator too," she said in a deadpan eastern European accent.

"Twenty-five and one hundred," I murmured, shaking my head the moment I did.

"What this?" asked the woman.

"Floor three please," I said, trying to catch my breath.

The woman didn't move a muscle, not even changing the expression on her face. The boy reached forward and happily hit the button.

"We not take order from people," the woman admonished the boy. The boy blushed.

"Guarda che tette ha questo sloveno!"[82] declared Benito.

---

[82] Look at the tits this Slovenian has.

"Molto meglio delle tue tette cadenti, vecchia stronza,"[83] answered the woman.

Benito looked like he was going to cry. I politely looked down at my shoes. The boy picked his nose. The door opened on the third floor. I hustled Benito out before he could say anything more. Luck was with us. Father Jim was about to head down the escalator on the other side of the balcony which rounded the lobby. He had Agatha Christie tucked in his arms.

"Father Jim!" I called, not daring to raise my voice.

He didn't hear.

"Father Jim!" I called out a bit louder.

He stepped onto the escalator.

"I've been sitting on my ass waiting for you!" yelled Benito at the top of his lungs.

Father Jim and pretty much everyone else within earshot looked at us. I waved my arms. His gaze found us and then he turned and ran back up the escalator, pushing a couple of ladies in large shouldered blazers out of the way. We started hustling, making our way around the balcony, meeting him halfway around.

"How did you get the dog?" I asked.

Agatha Christie growled at me. Father Jim's face was set in stone.

"I handled it."

"What do you mean?" I asked.

"I handled it," Father Jim firmly repeated.

"Penso che il topo nero abbia ucciso quella donna,"[84] offered Benito.

"We need to hurry," I said. "Those two goons are in the building."

"How did they get past security?"

---

[83] Much better than your saggy tits, you old bitch.
[84] I think the black rat killed that woman.

"They gave him a Ulysses S. Grant."

The priest smacked his head with the palm of his hand. I could hear him say of course in my head even though he never did.

"We need to get this done," I reminded him.

Father Jim nodded.

"This way. I saw a place."

Part 17 - L'esorcismo

The room was not a big one, mostly storage for stacked chairs and round tables on their sides with folded legs. Father Jim was doing knee bends and other such stretches. Benito was nervously pacing back and forth. Agatha Christie was peeing on a stack of chairs.

"Finalmente questo incubo può finire."[85]

Footsteps approached the closed door. We all froze. Agatha Christie growled. The footsteps continued down the hallway.

"Can we get this done?" I insisted.

I felt like I could run to the moon and back I was so anxious. Father Jim continued with his stretches.

"It never hurts to be limber," he replied in the middle of his lunges. "Do you have a bottle?"

"What do you mean a bottle?"

"We need a container," he explained. "The one I had was in my bag."

"Frick," I said.

"Language."

---

[85] Finally this nightmare can end.

"We lost your bag."

"I know we lost my bag," he answered.

Father Jim paused to give me a look, like I was being stupid, and then went back to his lunges. More footsteps came down the hall. Again we all froze, except for that damnable Agatha Christie who loped towards the door, their hackles raised, growling. The footsteps moved on. Father Jim was doing a bicep stretch behind his back.

"We need a container," he repeated.

"You don't listen too good, do ya, asshole?" said Benito.

I let out an audible sigh, went up to the door, and pressed my ear against it to listen.

"Once you step out of the sunlight into the narrow corridors, it's time to protect your nuts guys," said Benito.

I gave him a dirty look. I cracked open the door and peeked out. The hallway was empty. I waited. Listening.

"Ti comporti come se fossi nel corpo della vecchia signora,"[86] laughed Benito.

I didn't like his tone. I rolled my eyes at him and went into the hallway. A sweating portly man in a shirt and tie was already halfway down the hall. Shit.

"Were there any jugs for the water cooler in there?" he jovially asked as he approached.

I stared at him blankly. He came to rest next to me, smiling a toothy grin.

"No," I said, trying to sound casual, but just stretching out the word beyond the norm.

"Are you sure?" he asked, his eyes lasered to the door.

I could hear Agatha Christie growling on the other side of the door.

"Did you hear something?" asked the portly man, looking at me.

"I think they're vacuuming somewhere."

---

[86] You're acting like you're in the old lady body.

The portly man harumphed.

"They're not supposed to be vacuuming until the evening."

I shrugged.

"Maybe they made a mess."

The portly man chuckled.

"Those wild accountants," he said with a wink.

I didn't know what to say, so I just gave him a smile.

"Are you sure there's no water bottles?" he asked.

"Positive," I answered.

"Maybe I should check," he said, trying to shift his bulk around me.

"Are you calling me a liar," I demanded.

The portly man ceased his forward momentum. He seemed flustered.

"Of course not."

"Because from where I'm standing it looks like you're calling me an asshole," I insisted.

The portly man was really sweating.

"I'm sorry," he said. "I guess I can go check on four."

"You better," I said.

He gave me a bit of a look but started shuffling off. At the corner he turned and gave me a second look, so I just glared at him and gave him the old two fingers towards my eyes then towards him routine. This really seemed to fluster him and he disappeared around the corner.

You don't really need to hear about the rest of the trials I had to go through to find a container, because it was actually quite easy. Down the hall was a conference room with a table covered in various snacks, coffee urns, and best of all, large bowls of ice with bottles of pop. I grabbed a Diet Coke, took a swig from it, dumped the rest in a nearby potted plant, and made my way back to the storage room.

Father Jim was ready to go when I got back. He was holding Agatha Christie in his arms and cooing softly to her.

Judging by how her tail was wagging she seemed to be enjoying it. Benito was scowling in the corner. I handed over the bottle and Father Jim took it without a word. He started the process.

I don't need to go into it. Father Jim was completely right. It was most definitely gross. More than gross, it was stomach churning disturbing. Agatha Christie started yelping horribly about halfway through, their little dog body twitching in all sorts of horrible ways in time with the steady cadence of Father Jim's quiet incantations. The priest's eyes were rolled up into the back of his head. I looked over at Benito. His eyes were wide with terror.

"Porca miseria!"[87] he screamed.

The yelping grew louder. The scene became more horrific. I covered my eyes, but I could feel the terrible energy of the room. I could feel the churning vortex fueled by Father Jim's steady litany clawing its way through the air, searching and seeking, gaining purchase for a moment within me, trying to latch hold, cold claws scraping across me as they were pulled across and away from me. It felt like my very soul was loosened, my body's hold upon it more tenuous than before. Tears were streaming down my face. I fell to my knees.

"Preferirei essere una vecchia signora con le tette cadenti!"[88]

I heard orthopedic shoes rapidly shuffling away. I heard the door open and close. There was nothing that could be done. I was frozen with fear. I was scared to death that even the slightest movement might lead to me being swept away. There was a terrible gagging and slurping sound, and then nothing. It was all gone. I was just in a storage room once again.

---

[87] Pig misery!
[88] I'd rather be an old lady with saggy tits!

I opened my eyes. Father Jim was holding what appeared to be a full bottle of Diet Coke and breathing heavily. Peaches was curled up on the floor, panting heavily and whimpering. Father Jim twisted the plastic cap onto the bottle.

"Where's Benito?" he demanded.

All I could do was shrug.

"Fuck!"

He rose up and swiftly moved toward the door, bottle in hand, leaving Peaches where he lay.

"C'mon," he ordered, "we have to find her!"

As it turned out, Benito wasn't all that hard to find. The body of an old lady, even one inhabited by the spirit of a dead fascist dictator, apparently is not the best vehicle for a quick getaway. We found him cowering behind the craft services table in the very room where I had found the bottle of Diet Coke. His body's varicose veined legs and orthopedic shoes were sticking out far enough for us to see them as we passed by the open doorway. He rose up when he heard us rush in. His face was white and his eyes were huge and full of fear.

"Vaffanculo!"[89] he screamed, tears running down his cheeks.

Father Jim rushed forward and manhandled him to the ground behind the table.

"I have the rights to a lawyer!" screamed Benito. "I have right to a lawyer!"

"Get her mouth opened," ordered Father Jim.

I did as I was told. I don't really want to go into it. Have you ever been involved in forcing an old lady to drink an entire bottle of what looks like Diet Coke but is actually her own soul? Well I have, and it was just the frosting on an already shit filled cake. When all of it was

---

[89] Fuck you!

119

down, Benito let out a terrible high pitched throaty scream and began convulsing. Father Jim held them tight and began his incantations.

"Margaret Thatcher's juicy jubblies?!"

I staggered up from behind the table. Nigel and The Grip were in the doorway. Father Jim, still out of sight, began to increase the rhythm and volume of his incantations. I could feel the vile fingers begin to try and find purchase yet again.

"What's all this then?" yelled Nigel.

He and The Grip began to reach into their jacket pockets for their guns. I didn't hesitate. I didn't even think. I leaped over the table, spilling a platter of Minnesota sushi across the floor. I rushed across the space between us in record time. I threw myself against the two of them, catching both off balance, propelling them back out into the hallway and onto the floor where we fell in a tangled heap.

"Dirty flap slapper!" yelled Nigel.

The Grip just kept snickering. It was creepy as all get out. He was the first to regain his feet. He grabbed me by my belt, lifted me like a ragdoll, and threw me into the wall. I mean literally into the wall. The fricking thing buckled and I left a roughly me shaped divot. It hurt like hell. I mean, have you ever been thrown into a wall? It's not great.

Nigel rose to his knees. Out of the corner of my eye, I caught sight of someone rounding the corner down the hall, pausing, and then rushing off. A muffled scream came from the conference room. Both Nigel and The Grip swung their oversized heads in that direction. I screamed at the top of my lungs, hoping it would drown out all else, and threw myself at Nigel, catching him off balance again. His head collided with the door frame with a solid thwack and he went limp under me.

The Grip caught me by the belt again and hucked me into the conference room like an oversized bowling ball. It felt only marginally better than getting thrown into the wall. He was smiling at me with his terrible metallic golden smile, the black gap looming large. He reached into his jacket pocket and pulled out his snubbed nosed pistol. He pointed it at me. The black gap loomed larger. The muffled screams and Father Jim's incantations seemed very far away. I closed my eyes, waiting for the bullet.

The Grip screamed like a little girl. It was possibly the highest pitched scream I've ever heard come out of a man, and that's really saying something. I opened my eyes to see him spinning like a fricking dervish, Peaches firmly attached to his bloody gun hand. The Jack Russell's little body stretched out straight as an arrow from the centrifugal force, droplets of slobber and blood pinwheeling outward. Where the frick was the gun?! Peaches lost his grip and went flying toward me, thunking down right into my lap. The Grip let out another high pitched banshee howl full of rage and rushed toward us, his eyes those of a shark hunting its prey.

The world seemed to slow down.

Father Jim popped up from behind the table, screwing the cap back onto the seemingly now full again bottle of Diet Coke. Without a moment's hesitation he leapt across the table, scattering the two bowls of ice and pop as he went. Peaches cowered in my arms. Father Jim, bottle of Mussolini still in his hand, slammed into The Grip right as the monstrous pale figure was about to reach Peaches and me. The two bulky boys slammed into the floor together and then scrambled to regain their feet.

Father Jim rose first. He swung a meaty fist into The Grip's mouth, punching a fresh gap into the golden grill. The Grip laughed and clawed at Father Jim, using the priest to lever himself upward, ripping open Father Jim's shirt, sending buttons and his white priest collar flying. The Grip head butted Father Jim. The priest staggered, pulling The Grip down with him as he fell. The bottle of Diet Coke containing what I hoped was the soul of Benito Mussolini rolled free from the melee. I shoved Peaches off my lap and scrambled forward on my hands and knees to grab it. Peaches started barking from the corner of the room.

"Enough ya twats!" yelled Nigel.

He strode through the doorway, his pistol ranging back and forth, trying to decide where to shoot first. Peaches kept barking. I rose, my hands slightly raised, holding the bottle of Diet Coke. Father Jim had gained the upper hand again, up on his knees with The Grip flat on his back beneath him. He punched The Grip hard in the face, but then saw the gun. He stopped. He rose slowly, his hands well away from his sides but not up. The Grip lifted himself up. His face was bloody and swollen. He cheap shotted Father Jim right in the gut and then limped over to stand next to his comrade in gooning. Father Jim doubled over and wheezed, but he did not fall.

"Put that down ya chav," ordered Nigel, gesturing at the bottle of Diet Coke in my hand.

I set it down on the edge of the table.

"I've had just about enough of this crazy ass shite," declared Nigel.

The Grip wiped his mouth with the back of his hand and gave a wincing snicker. Nigel's whole body seemed to shake.

"I need some bloody answers. This whole thing has been tits up since..."

He fell silent. We all heard what he heard. Even Peaches stopped barking. The sharp clipping sounds of high heels were moving down the hallway. Father Jim and I looked at each other. Nigel tucked the hand holding his gun under his jacket and gave us a threatening look.

A chicly dressed blonde woman in a striped blouse and pencil skirt came into the room. Her Buddy Holly glasses and hair up in a tight bun gave her an air of competent authority. She paused in the doorway, taking it all in, and then walked forward. All of us subconsciously moved out of her way.

"Straight one hundred," murmured Father Jim.

Nigel shot him a warning look.

"Are you with the TV crew?" she demanded.

We all looked at each other. Nigel smacked his lips and took in a breath.

"Uh, yes ma'am, that's right ma'am," he said, "we're with the telly crew."

The woman gazed around the room again.

"What happened in here?"

We all looked at each other again. The Grip snickered a bit but winced when he did.

"It was like that when we came in here," Nigel answered.

The woman pursed her lips, obviously not believing us. Peaches yipped from the corner.

"Is that Kylie's dog?"

"I think so," I answered, not sure why I answered.

"Fucking Kylie," said the woman.

She looked around again and then strode to the table and picked up the bottle of Diet Coke. My breath hissed inward and I could hear Father Jim's do the same.

"I don't have time for this shit," she proclaimed to no one in particular. "Get this all cleaned up or I don't care what union you're part of, you'll all be out on your asses faster than you can say Jumping Jack Flash juggles junked jalopies in Japan."

"Yes ma'am," said Nigel, dipping his head obediently.

The woman strode from the room. We could hear her high heels clicking down the hall. My entire body was shaking. I would have rushed after her right then and there, but Nigel pulled back out his gun. He took in a deep breath and let it out. He was sweating profusely.

"Now I'm not gonna to ask ya again," he stated, his voice flat, "and if I don't get an answer there's goin to be one of ya with more holes than ya had before."

The Grip didn't snicker this time, but the pure elation he was evidently feeling was written all over his face.

"So then," continued Nigel, "where in the bloody hell is Annis?"

"I'm right here," answered Agatha Christie, rising up from behind the table.

Nigel jumped with such surprise I was worried the gun might go off. The Grip remained nonchalant. Agatha Christie gestured at the gun in Nigel's hand.

"Put that bloody thing away, ya twat."

"We thought…" started the flabbergasted Nigel.

"I've never seen any evidence that my niece's boyfriend pays ya idiots to think," she interrupted.

Nigel obediently shut his mouth. Agatha Christie gestured at Father Jim.

"Hand me that dog."

Father Jim did as he was told. He picked up Peaches, walked over to Agatha Christie, handed him to her across the table, and then stepped back. Peaches growled a bit, but Agatha Christie gave him a light thump on the nose and he quit.

"Quit fussing," she ordered. "I'm not going back in."

"I thought ya hated dags?" said Nigel.

"I'm rather attached to this one," she said. "Not that it's any of your business, ya tosser."

Nigel turned red and looked down at his shoes.

"Are we free to go?" asked Father Jim.

"No one has a gun on ya," replied Agatha Christie.

Nigel and The Grip looked confused, but they kept silent. Father Jim and I started toward the door.

"You promised triple," said Agatha Christie, her eyes boring into me.

"Of course," I said.

She nodded. I nodded back. Father Jim and I hustled from the room. The moment we got to the hallway we began to run, praying fervently that we'd be able to find the woman before anything else could go wrong.

Part 18 - Uomo nel Parco

Our prayers must have worked.

"There she is!" called out Father Jim, rushing toward the nearest escalator without even waiting to see if I had heard him.

We were on the third floor balcony, each of us on either side of the open expanse, our eyes roving the world below. The woman was down on the main floor, just passing through one of the golden revolving doors leading to the street outside. The Diet Coke was clutched casually in her hand by the cap, still full. Thank God still full. I rushed toward the nearest escalator on my side. Across the way I could see Father Jim already descending the far escalator, pushing people out of the way.

"Get out of the fricking way!" I yelled as I began my own descent.

It's amazing when you look frantic and sleep deprived, and mix in some top of the lung screaming, how many people do as they're told. It's also amazing how many are so caught up in their own worlds, most with chines tucked down, eyes on at their phones, that they don't notice a damn thing. These were the ones who forcefully prodded out of the way by my skinny sharp elbows, a gift which had always seemed like a detriment up until that moment. Not to self-aggrandize too much, but I'm pretty sure my sharp elbows were the reason Father Jim and I reached the revolving front door at the same time.

When we got outside we had no idea where to look. The streets and sidewalks were crowded, people hustling and bustling on their own adventures. She was gone. Not sure what else to do, I spun around ineffectually, trying to magically pierce the mass of bodies.

"Get on my shoulders," yelled Father Jim.

I didn't even pause to make a snide remark. He squatted down, I climbed onto his shoulders like an excited toddler, and up I went, towering above the crowds. Father Jim began to spin slowly and my head whipped around, looking desperately for the woman.

"There she is!" I yelled.

She was crossing the street two blocks away. Father Jim spun to align himself with the pointing compass of my finger and then started to run with me still on his shoulders, dancing his ways through the crowd. My heart was pounding in my ears and I was thrown this way and that, gripping his mammoth neck with my spindly legs, his big hands encircling my shins. For a moment he stumbled and we nearly went down.

"You're going to choke me out!" he yelled.

I loosened my legs and on we went, careening up the street. A man operating a hot dog cart laughed uproariously.

"Only in New York," the man yelled to the people waiting in line.

"Fucking Voltron!" screamed a homeless man, shaking his fist with unbridled rage.

When we reached the crosswalk where we had last seen her, traffic moving and there was no way to reasonably move forward. On the other side was Central Park. There was a golden statue of a man on a horse.

"I bet that horse has an asshole," quipped Father Jim, breathing heavily. "The best statues always have well sculpted assholes."

I chose to say nothing. It was a really weird thing to bring up, especially at a time like this. My eyes were searching. Then I saw her, moving along the edge of the park and then turning deeper into it down a flight of stairs.

"I see her!" I yelled. "Go straight!"

Father Jim answered by shifting me higher on his shoulders and pushing his way forward to the edge of the sidewalk. The light changed. The walk sign turned to the walking man. Father Jim hustled across the street, the pedestrians coming in either direction clearing space around us like fish around a whale.

"Right!" I yelled when we reached the stairs.

Father Jim nimbly spun right on the toe tips of a single foot and down the stairs we went.

"Shit!" I yelled as I caught a face full of branches.

Down I went. They weren't thick branches, and Father Jim partially caught me as I fell, so it didn't hurt all that much. But still it cost us precious seconds to get ourselves sorted out.

"Are you okay?" asked Father Jim.

"Go!" I yelled as he wrenched me to my feet.

So we went, running together, coming out at a large pond ringed by a path and various greenery bursting with spring freshness. The woman was down the way a bit, maybe forty yards away, approaching a heavy set man sitting on a park bench. He had on an oversized suit and sported an elaborate comb over. Three empty Big Mac boxes were next to him on the bench, with only half of one still in his hand. You would know him if you saw him. He was a big reality TV star at the time. I don't dare say who given how much they like to sue.

The woman walked up to him. His beady eyes hungrily gave her the up and down as though he wanted to devour her like the burger in his hand. She said something to him and handed him the Diet Coke. He burped, said something back to her, and took the bottle. He opened it and raised it to his lips.

"No!" Father Jim and I screamed in unison.

Who knows if the woman or reality star heard us, at least if they did they gave no sign to understanding it had anything to do with them. Who did hear us was the gang of well dressed security guards who descended on us, throwing us to the ground. I was easy, but it took four of them to dogpile Father Jim. Their leader was talking on a radio pulled from his belt. With our faces in the gravel of the path we watched the man drink down the entire Diet Coke in one long pull. It was kind of impressive.

We heard him make a loud grunting sound like a man having a heart attack, and watched him twitch, then shake as though he felt a sudden chill. The woman leaned over and seemed to be asking if he was all right. He raised a hand, seemingly to cut her off, and then went back to eating his hamburger. The head security guard jogged over and said something to the man. The man looked back and gave a little smile. He finished his hamburger. He got up, slow to lift his bulk, and shambled up the path, the head security guard and the woman following in his wake. The man got to us. He bent down at us and leaned in close.

"There are three ways to win," he whispered. "One, you knock the guy out. Two, your opponent quits and shouts, matte. It's like saying uncle. Three, you throw the fucker right off the runway."

The man gave us a smile and raised his eyebrows and then let them fall.

"Siete dei perdenti,"[90] he snarled.
He walked away without looking back.

---

[90] You're losers.

Benito

Part 19 - Anatre

The security guards held us until the police arrived, who then in turn questioned us for a while, waited for the security guards to leave, and then just let us go. Apparently, it's not a crime to run screaming through Central Park.

"If it was," the police sergeant said, "we'd have half this damn city locked up."

Free again, Father Jim and I sat down on the park bench where the three empty hamburger boxes had been left behind.

"What are we going to do?" I asked. "Maybe we could sneak back into the building..."

Father Jim shrugged.

"Be pretty hard with all the security," he said. "Especially now that they've marked us."

"We've got to do something. I mean, this guy has money and a huge TV audience. That can't be a good combination."

Father Jim just shrugged again.

"I don't know. The guy's kind of a joke."

I tried to think of something else to say.

"Besides," he continued. "I've got to get back before Sunday. The daily mass is one thing, but if I'm not there for Sunday mass then one of the busy bodies will complain to the Bishop and then there will be all sorts of heck to pay."

I didn't say anything. I just stared out at a line of ducks swimming on the pond.

"Don't you have a job or something you need to get back to?" he asked.

I nervously laughed and gave him my best smile.

"I'm definitely not making internet videos of stomping on birthday cakes," I blurted.

Father Jim narrowed his eyes and bit his lower lip. I could feel myself turning red.

"At least not anymore," I added.

Father Jim was blushing too, clear to his ears. He did the sign of the cross.

"At least I have something on Mindy Gabaldon," I said.

"Who's Mindy Gabaldon?"

I opened my mouth to explain but then shut it. Father Jim looked at me with his damnable serenely patient face, waiting longer than was normal. Luckily even he had his limits, finally looking away and back toward the pond when he figured out I probably wasn't going to answer. It didn't really matter who Mindy Gabaldon was. And besides, if she was stomping on cakes she would most definitely be doing it better. The little minx has the cutest little feet, the kind most cake stomping enthusiasts just love.

One of the ducks out on the pond let out a series of quacks.

"Can I ask you something?" I asked.

"Sure," answered Father Jim, still staring out at the ducks.

"How did you really get that dog from Kylie M.? I've been dying to know."

Father Jim took in a breath and let it out.

"I don't really want to talk about it."

"Did you rough her up a bit or something?"

I elbowed him good naturedly. Father Jim rubbed his big hands on his thick thighs.

"I flirted with her," he answered.

"You flirted with her?" I repeated.

Father Jim gave a little smirk.

"It's hard to imagine a priest lying," he said. "And I did say I'd bring the dog back."

"So that's it then?"

He kept his eyes on the ducks.

"Some women really like muscular men."

He paused.

"Two temptations in a single day might have been a little too much."

For perhaps the first time in my life I kept my mouth shut, and for that I was rewarded. The silence dragged on for what felt like an excruciating amount of time, but it ended with Father Jim continuing.

"I told her I needed to borrow her dog. I flashed her a smile when I did, held myself up nice and tight. People like that kind of thing. I told her I was on my way to visit a man whose mother had recently died, that he needed a bit of cheering up, and that he loved dogs. Then she told me her cousin had been molested by a priest. She didn't sound angry. She just said it. I don't know why she just blurted it out, but some people feel the need to tell stories like that to any one of us they meet. To remind us. I felt the shame many of us do when we hear such things. When I asked how long ago, she said not long. When I asked how old he had been, she said middle aged. He had been a deacon, shy and soft-spoken. The priest had touched him and her cousin had done nothing to stop it. He had no idea how to stop it. I didn't know what to say, and I'm ashamed to say my first thought was to grab the dog and run away. That's when she kissed me. Why did she do that? It made no sense. I thought about stopping her, but I didn't. I started kissing her back. Then my arms were around her. Then my hands were on her chest. You're checking a lot of my boxes she said."

Father Jim fell silent again. His eyes were watery. I sat perfectly still, neither leaning toward him or away from him.

"And after that, I don't know," he said, "but I got the dog, and that's the important part.

His big hands were clasped tightly in front of him. He was staring at them.

"I don't understand people at all," he muttered, then lapsed back into silence.

Another duck let out a series of quacks.

"So you're saying you're going to have to do a whole lot of pushups?" I asked.

Father Jim gave an appreciative grunt, a faint smile on his lips.

"So many."

We both gazed out at the pond. One of the male ducks, I'm not sure what you call a male duck, separated one of the female ducks from the rest. She made cranky duck sounds at him, but he ignored her.

"Do you really think we should do nothing?" I asked.

Father Jim shrugged. The female duck was trying to get around the male duck, making angrier duck sounds, but he kept at it, driving her into the shallows.

"Maybe it's God's plan," he suggested.

I picked up a handful of rocks and hucked them at the male duck, creating little splashes around him.

"Get away from her you rapist!" I yelled.

One rock hit home, striking the male duck on his back. He threw himself into the air with a perturbed quack. I could feel Father Jim staring at me.

"Ducks are designed around rape," I explained. "The females have maze vaginas with passages they can open and close to keep themselves from getting pregnant when they don't want to be and the male duck has a long corkscrew dick he uses to try and force his way in."

"I thought birds had cloacas," said Father Jim.

"Not ducks. My friend Emily told me all about it. She's really into ducks."

The female duck was swimming back to be with her fellows. The male duck I scared away had landed and was swimming in the same direction. None of the other ducks seemed to care one way or another.

"Do you think saying it's God's plan is just an excuse to do nothing?" I asked.

Father Jim shrugged.

"Does it matter if there's nothing you can do?" he asked.

I didn't know how to answer, so I just shrugged too.

Benito

Part 20 - La Benedizione

There isn't much to tell about the train ride back home.
Both Father Jim and I slept a good chunk of the trip, and the
parts we didn't sleep we mostly spent debating which giant
multinational corporate conglomeration makes the best
chocolate milk. When we got back home we said our
goodbyes and Father Jim gave me a big bear hug, Father Jim
gives a pretty damn good bear hug. Then he got into the taxi
I bought for him and headed back to the rectory. He
suggested we share, but I told him it was all right, I needed
some me time. I rode a series of buses to get back home.

Life went on. Mindy Gabaldon got to play Captain
Hook after all, rolling about on stage in a wheelchair. All the
local theater blogs raved about it, calling the portrayal of a
disabled Captain Hook both a heart-rending new look at an
old character and a brave new chapter in repertory
theater. Of course only Mindy Gabaldon could pull off
pretending to be disabled while only temporarily disabled
and not offend anyone. The woman is a damn firecracker.

Agatha Christie started showing up at my apartment
after being M.I.A. for a few weeks. One day there was a

knock on the door, and there she was, frumpily dressed and scowling as always, pretty much pretending that nothing had happened, though she did bring Peaches with her. As soon as I let her in she marched over to my liquor collection.

"Es this one all right ya slag?" she asked, lifting and shaking a bottle of vodka.

I nodded. She carried the bottle into the kitchen and made herself a drink.

"The bathroom is pretty dirty," I said.

"I bet it es," she called back from the kitchen.

Peaches lifted a leg and peed on the side of my couch. The little Jack Russell had a very self-satisfied look on his face when he did it.

"Your dog peed on my couch," I called into the kitchen.

"He does that," she answered.

"Are you going to at least clean it?"

She didn't bother to answer. When she left, I paid her the triple rate, just as we had agreed. What else could I do?

The next day I went out and bought some cakes to stomp on for some extra cash. For whatever reason bar mitzvah cakes are really big in the stomping community right now. No idea why. The cake stomping community is weird.

Teddy never got back to me, though I did try calling and texting him several more times.

"I bet Dr. Pepper only has a doctorate in communications or something stupid like that," I could hear him say when the electronic voice told me his voicemail was full. "What a phony."

As for Emily, she did eventually text me, asking if I wanted to join her at some hip bar to watch The Bachelor. I went, and to her credit she didn't bring up the whole dog biting her thing. But while we talked she did tell me this long convoluted story that ended with her not being able to go within a thousand yards of a school anymore. Soon after that I made an excuse to go home early. I haven't really hung out with her since.

Life went on, as they do, and then one day I saw on social media that the reality star had announced that he was getting into politics. My hands were shaking so hard it was tough to see the video of him descending that golden escalator. I tried phoning Father Jim, but he didn't answer. The next day I went to morning mass at his church.

I was a little late, but only because the bus was delayed, so I snuck quietly in and sat down in the back. I was the youngest one there by a good thirty to forty years. The old gray heads were all bent low as Father Jim led them in prayers. Father Jim looked a bit unsure when he saw me come in, but he didn't miss a beat. I rose and sat and kneeled whenever the old timers did. When they lined up to get their free bread and wine, I joined them too. Father Jim didn't give me any bread or wine, but he did bless me, which though I don't believe in such things, was still pretty nice of him. When the service was done, I waited in my pew while Father Jim shook hands and said goodbye to his parishioners. When he was done he led me through a side door into the rectory. It was different than before. Less workout equipment and a bunch of yoga mats stacked in a corner.

"I'm trying to learn to be more flexible," he explained.

We went into the kitchen where he opened the fridge and pulled out a sheet cake. Happy Bat Matzvah Abner it said on it. He cut off a big slice and gestured at me with the knife.

"Want one?" he asked.

He had a little smile that told me that he knew what the answer was, but that he was just poking at me a bit. But not in an unfriendly way.

"No thank you," I said, giving him a smile back.

He put the sheet cake back and started to eat.

"Did you see the news?" I asked.

"You mean that white lady in Washington who was pretending to be black?" asked Father Jim.

"Benito," I said, only slightly annoyed.

"Oh yeah, crazy stuff."

His mouth was full, so I waited to see if he would say anything more. Instead he just put another big bite of cake into his mouth.

"Doesn't it worry you?" I asked.

Father Jim shrugged.

"Not really much we could do about it. Besides, the guy's a bit of a joke."

I watched him eat. My hands were clenched.

"What if we could get the help of somebody who could do something about it?"

"Like who?" he asked through a mouthful of cake.

I gave him a look. Father Jim didn't notice at first, but when he did, he grew somber. He swallowed and put the plate down on the kitchen counter.

"That would be a bad idea," he said quietly.

"We don't have a lot of other options."

"You never get out of a mess the same way you get into it."

We stared at each other.

"I have to do something," I said.

Father Jim sighed.

"Wait here."

He went back into the church. When he came back he was holding one of the little pieces of bread.

"Take this," he ordered.

I took it from him, trying my best not to roll my eyes.

"How can you do nothing?" I insisted.

He said a little blessing.

"Don't eat it," he ordered.

I ate it on the bus ride home.

Part 21 - Il Ritorno

Ironically, it was the same Lyft driver as the time before. I'm not sure if I'm using ironically correctly, but I don't really care. Either way, he looked about as pleased to see me as I was to see him.

"Are you going to give me one star again?" he demanded.

"Are you going to leave me in the middle of nowhere again?" I countered.

"You promised no funny business."

"Fuck you."

"No, screw you," he answered.

We both stared at each other, him in his car and me on the sidewalk.

"How about I promise five stars no matter what this time?" I asked.

"And a big tip too?" he insisted.

"And a big tip too," I promised.

We rode pretty much the whole way in silence, only breaking it once for him to ask me whether or not I would like to listen to the radio. When I said okay, he turned on

NPR. I was fairly surprised, he didn't seem the type. When we got to the crossroads I had him park a little way back, just like before. I don't think I need to explain the lead up from here. It was basically the same as last time, with the Devil stepping out from behind the signpost in the exact same outfit, only now without the t-shirt, just bare chested under his black pleather vest, his chest smooth except for a little tuft and some prominently long nipple hairs.

"You again?" he said. "Tell your buddy Teddy that dirt bike already crapped out."

"I haven't talked to him in a while," I answered.

His cat eyes narrowed.

"Whatever. What in the heck do you want?"

I braced myself. I took in a breath and let it out. My shoulders rose involuntarily.

"I want to make a deal."

The Devil cackled.

"Haven't we already done this?"

"I need your help with Benito."

The Devil cackled even louder, bending over with his mirth.

"You think you'd know better after all the problems you caused," he said. "I mean, I couldn't have come up with half the chaos you've caused by sheer ineptitude."

"Please," I said, "I'll do anything."

"Oh, I'm sure of that," said the Devil, straightening and wiping away a laughter tear.

I tried not to imagine the terrible things one might be asked for by the Devil. I mean, I've lived a life, but even I historically had my limits.

"Whatever needs to be done," I assured him.

His mouth bent into a quivering smirk. He looked like he was about to start cackling again, but he didn't.

"Look," he said holding up a hand. "First," one finger rose with a long grimy fingernail, "you still don't have anything I want which I probably won't eventually get. This present bout of virtuous self-sacrifice notwithstanding."

He leered at me and mimed stomping on a cake with his boots, making squishing sounds with his mouth.

"Second," he said, holding up a second finger with an equally long and grimy nail, "why would I want to ruin all the fun?"

He had perhaps the widest smile I've ever seen across his face.

"And third," he began, holding up a third finger, this one with a perfectly manicured nail, "that Subway card you gave me did not have a free six inch on it."

The Devil's smile was getting bigger and bigger, but his eyes were deadly serious.

"Do you have any idea how embarrassing that is? You made me look like an idiot in front of Mitch, my favorite sandwich artist."

His mouth covered more than half his face. He took a step toward me. I was terrified, but rooted to the spot, unable to move a muscle.

"A sandwich artist won't make you the best sandwich if they don't take you seriously," insisted the Devil.

He took another step toward me. His eyes seemed to be on fire. His mouth grew wider and wider. His neck lengthened and elongated, bending at an unnatural angle. I could see clear down to his stomach, which was full of flames, worms, and screaming people. His hot Cool Ranch Dorito breath blasted across my face. I didn't breathe. Closer he came, and still I couldn't move a muscle. His jaw unhinged. My heart stopped beating. I knew he was preparing to consume me in a single gulp.

A shot rang out.

The Devil staggered, a bullet wound in the middle of his chest. Another shot rang out, and then another, both striking close to the first in a beautiful grouping. The Devil leaned back on his heels, for a moment he teetered there, and then he fell with his back straight as a board. The moment he fell, I slumped as though I was a marionette that had just had its strings cut.

I looked behind me. The Lyft driver was out of his car and holding his gun, using the side mirror to steady his arm. As I watched, he rose from his semi-crouched position and came forward, never moving his gun off the collapsed form in front of us.

"Nice shot," I said, struggling to catch my breath.

"I told you I was fast," he said.

When he drew even, he gave the Devil's boot a kick with his shoe. The Devil didn't respond.

"I didn't like the look of him at all," said the Lyft driver.

"Thank you," I said.

"In this world, we all have to do what we can for each other," he answered.

He had a bit of a smile on his lips.

"Even if the other guy is an asshole," he added.

I got out my phone and gave him his five stars and a big tip right then and there. It was really the least I could do.

"Do you like waffles?" I asked.

"Who doesn't like waffles?" he answered.

On the way back we stopped for waffles. My treat. Over the course of the meal it became apparent that he was a huge homophobe and transphobe. Go figure. At least the waffles were pretty good.

Benito

Also Written By The Author

The Uncanny Valley

We all know a Paul. A person who seems to see stuff that isn't there. The type the polite call quirky and the blunt call nuts. Conspiracies? He's got a few. He's got his finger on how the world really works. He knows what kind of shit is coming down the pipe. Flee across the West Texas desert to Mexico? Makes sense to him. Feel like you're being watched? You bet your ass someone is watching. Best turn off your cellphone. Troubles? Of course, that's just part of life. Doubts? No time for doubts. Shit is getting real. Get in, buckle up, crack open a beer. The only real question is, how far down the rabbit hole are you willing to follow?

An Unsated Thirst

They say that an author's first stories are their most raw. Here is a collection of S.W. Campbell's first short stories and writings. Combining both published and unpublished works, An Unsated Thirst explores victory and defeat, triumph and shame, and an unflinching view of our naked selves. How one views such stories is dependent upon the mood of the reader. Whether we are at our highs or at our lows. However, it is hard for any of us to claim that such stories are ones that we cannot identify with. Contained within these pages are parts of our lives which we try to forget, though they are an important part of what makes us whole. Such stories should be embraced, accepted within ourselves so we can better accept them with others.

Papaya

When a devastating hurricane hits the Caribbean island of Domenique, its inhabitants are forced into a singular struggle to survive and rebuild. Isolated in their midst is Ted, a Peace Corps volunteer who fled the ashes of his former life only to find himself labeled an outsider. Infatuated by the enigmatic wife of his only friend, Ted thrusts himself into a world beyond his comprehension. As obsession turns to desperation, tensions grow and Ted is forced to decide exactly how far he will go to rebuild amidst the muddy ruins.

Stumptown

There are places where people say things are better. Where the downtowns do not empty after dark and people dare to dream beyond their means. Quirky utopias where the sins of the past are washed away by gentle rains and we all go forward arm in arm together into the brightening sunshine. Distant locations flocked to by young pilgrims, unencumbered by the deeply driven roots of age, where everything will be different. Combining both published and unpublished work, *Stumptown* is a collection of stories about ordinary people, navigating their personal anxieties and drama in a time when uncertainties were still tucked away and not allowed to distort the sense of hope in the air. It is a soliloquy to naivete, and the belief that a better world is a place rather than an idea.

The People's Republic of 47th & Long

Perhaps the world would be a better place if we thought of ourselves less as good people, and more as lousy people who manage to do good things. My friend Leopold was always a dreamer. The pandemic and our reactions to it left us broken and divided. Most of us just wanted to feel safe again, but others dreamt of something better. Leopold was one of these. Though I think he likely joined the People's Republic of 47th and Long purely out of geographic convenience, I know once part of it, he fully shared in its egalitarian vision. All I have are his letters. Sometimes I wish I had burned them, but I didn't, so now here they are. Maybe you can find a use for them. Perhaps they can help remind you who we truly are. The good, the bad, and most importantly, the indifferent.

The Man In The Sodden Cap

The Man In The Sodden Cap is a collection of twenty-six short stories written during a period of emotional unleashing, a madcap rush to get words to the page. As with any such period of unrelenting literary expulsion, the results are a mix of emotional, personal, poignant, and inane. For many authors, these are the types of stories that often get kept in a drawer somewhere, not shared with anyone. But what use are stories if they are not shared? Individually these are good stories, but taken all together they tell the tale of heartbreak and remorse, and the need to move on. In this context, The Man In A Sodden Cap is in many ways a sequel to S.W. Campbell's first short story collection, An Unsated Thirst, a continuation and fitting conclusion to that earlier work.

Senseless Sensibilities

It is the human condition to try and find meaning in this life, to make sense of the chaos and randomness around us. At times this need overwhelms common sense, building layers of cognitive dissonance until we are left running our lives based upon senseless sensibilities. Contained within these pages are thirty-six short stories which explore the ability of people to adapt and survive the world around them. Stories which provide insight into slices of existence, and which highlight the strange ridiculousness of everyday life. Whether it's an old man adapting his hobbies to his aging body, a commodities trader who finds himself to be the commodity, or a lonely man fulfilling two needs in a single cross-country trip, each shows the resilience and mental flexibility shared by us all.

The Lost Art of Initial Messaging

A long time ago, before the advent of matching and swiping, online dating was largely made up of random outreach and hoped for happenstance. In this chaotic milieu, a world of nothing but shots in the dark, a charming and witty initial message could mean the difference between meeting the love of your life and sadly sitting home alone in the dark, eating lukewarm soup. Part guidebook, part memoir, and part history lesson, *The Lost Art of Initial Messaging* tracks one man's attempts to find the perfect initial message. Contained within this book are unique jewels, lovingly crafted for each prospective mate. At times poignant, at times witty, and more often than not bordering on complete ridiculousness, each represent a valiant attempt to declare: I'm here. I see you. Do you see me too?

Trials and Tribulations

A long time ago, before the advent of matching and swiping, online dating was largely made up of random outreach and hoped for happenstance. In this chaotic milieu, a world of nothing but shots in the dark, a charming and witty initial message could mean the difference between meeting the love of your life and sadly sitting home alone in the dark, eating lukewarm soup. Part guidebook, part memoir, and part history lesson, *The Lost Art of Initial Messaging* tracks one man's attempts to find the perfect initial message. Contained within this book are unique jewels, lovingly crafted for each prospective mate. At times poignant, at times witty, and more often than not bordering on complete ridiculousness, each represent a valiant attempt to declare: I'm here. I see you. Do you see me too?

More information can be found at:

www.shawnwcampbell.com

Acknowledgements

A special thank you to Liz Knowles Ryan, Jane Mier Erwin, Brina Bolanz, Sumner Williams, Martin Epsil, Chad Holloway, Tracy Orvis, Katie Breene, and Kayla Barnes for their invaluable help in reading, proofreading, and providing notes for this story. Your input made it so much better and a bit of each of you is now part of it.

About The Author

S.W. Campbell was born in Eastern Oregon in 1983 after a harrowing drive through a fog. He currently resides in Portland, Oregon where he works as an economist and lives with a lovely house plant named Morton. He has had several short stories published in various literary reviews, some of which appear in this work, and has also self-published several books. His work can be found at www.shawnwcampbell.com.

www.ingramcontent.com/pod-product-compliance
Lightning Source LLC
Chambersburg PA
CBHW071342170626
46811CB00003B/954